ALSO BY ADRIANNA CUEVAS

The Total Eclipse of Nestor Lopez

CUBA
in my
POCKET

Adrianna Cuevas

FARRAR, STRAUS, GIROUX
NEW YORK

Farrar Straus Giroux Books for Young Readers
An imprint of Macmillan Publishing Group, LLC
120 Broadway, New York, NY 10271

mackids.com

Our books may be purchased in bulk for promotional,
educational, or business use. Please contact your local
bookseller or the Macmillan Corporate and Premium Sales
Department at (800) 221-7945 ext. 5442 or by email at
MacmillanSpecialMarkets@macmillan.com.

Library of Congress Cataloging-in-Publication Data is available.

ISBN 978-0-374-31467-5 (hardcover)

1   3   5   7   9   10   8   6   4   2

Printed in the United States of America by LSC Communications,
Harrisonburg, Virginia
First edition, 2021
Book design by Trisha Previte

To Dad, my hero
1945–2020

CHAPTER 1

Santa Clara, Cuba
April 1961

This is not my home.

Tía Carmen's kitchen doesn't have my model of a P-51 Mustang or scattered pieces of Erector set. Instead of a mango tree out front with a tocororo nest in its branches, there's a crowd of soldiers, slapping one another on the back and firing their rifles into the night air.

My cousin Manuelito slaps another domino down on the table. "Doble ocho, tonto," he cackles. His stubby fingers fidget over the remaining dominoes in front of him.

"Don't call me stupid," I say, narrowing my eyes.

Mami paces behind Manuelito, twisting a red dish towel in her hands. She reaches for the cross at her neck, and I hear her mumble the Lord's Prayer. "Padre nuestro, que está en el cielo."

Sharp shouts outside Tía Carmen's house cut off the rest of her prayer.

"Mami?"

My little brother, Pepito, starts to get up from his chair, but Mami puts her hand on his shoulder.

"Don't worry, nene. It's fine."

Mami and Tía Carmen exchange worried looks. They may be fooling Pepito, but they're not fooling me. Fidel's soldiers defeated a force of Cuban refugees who had fled to the United States and were trained by the American government. The refugees tried to invade Cuba at the Bay of Pigs, but Fidel's army quickly overtook them. From what Papi told me, this was our last hope of ridding our island of Fidel's oppressive government.

"Keep playing, Cumba," Mami says as she waves her hand at me. The candle on the table where Manuelito and I sit flickers, bouncing long shadows of dominoes across the plastic floral tablecloth.

I try to focus on the tile in my hand, but the shouting outside increases. I shake my head and slap another domino down on the table. "Tranque. I blocked you."

The waistband of my pants digs into my stomach, and I fidget in my folding chair. The chair squeaks, prompting Mami to give me a quick look from the window.

She dries the same bowl over and over until the dish towel is limp in her hands. Tía Carmen tries to turn the radio up, but Mami snaps the volume dial down.

"I don't want to listen to that foolishness," she mutters.

Manuelito looks at me from across the table. The light from the candle turns his eyebrows into thick brown triangles, and his fat cheeks cast a shadow on his neck.

"Your papi come home yet?" He sneers, and the candlelight elongates his front teeth into fangs.

Tía Carmen crosses the kitchen in a blur of blue cotton flowers. She slaps Manuelito on the back of the head, his neck snapping forward and flipping his brown hair into his eyes.

"Cállate, niño," she hisses.

Manuelito's being told to shut up offers little consolation. He doesn't know. He has no idea that at this moment, my papi is tucked in a corner of our house, hiding from Fidel's soldiers. He sent us to Tía Carmen's when Radio Rebelde blasted the news of the impending Yanqui invasion.

"I don't want you here if they come for me," he

said as he ruffled my hair, the smile on his lips failing to hide the nervousness in his eyes. Fidel's soldiers were rounding up anyone who had worked for former President Batista. Papi was a captain in the army. Even though he was just a lawyer in the Judge Advocate General's unit, those two bars on his uniform made him look important.

I wrap my feet around the legs of the folding chair to keep myself from kicking Manuelito. He's a year younger than I am, and he prides himself on being the most annoying eleven-year-old in the world.

Manuelito lowers his head closer to the table, his eyebrows thickening and his fangs growing longer. He whispers, "It's not gonna work, you know. Fidel always wins."

I unwrap my left foot from the chair and kick him in the shin. Manuelito winces. That was for Papi.

Tía Carmen turns up the radio by the sink, and Mami purses her lips. "¡Aquí, Radio Rebelde!" shouts a deep voice from the speaker. "The Yanqui imperialists have failed, are failing, and will fail to overthrow our glorious revolution!"

News of the Bay of Pigs invasion fills the kitchen. Fidel has been giving speech after speech, taunting the Cuban exiles and their American supporters.

The anthem of the 26th of July Movement, Fidel's government, blasts from the radio, and Mami turns it off.

I sigh. Manuelito, Pepito, and I try to concentrate on our domino game. But it's no use. You're supposed to play with four people. Normally, Papi would've been our fourth.

Pepito lays down a new domino, and his eyes grow wide. "¡Ay, caramba! ¡La caja de muertos!"

He slaps his hand over his mouth before Mami can hear him curse. Pepito has always thought the double-nine tile was bad luck because it's called the dead man's box. When I hear the stomps and shouts outside, I'm reminded that there are worse sources of bad luck than a little white tile.

"It's okay, hermanito. Don't worry," I reassure him.

I swipe my hand over the dominoes we've laid down, erasing our careful rows. Game over. I show Pepito how to line up the dominoes in front of one another and knock them down in a cascade. He claps his chubby hands and starts to set up the dominoes himself, sticking out his tongue in concentration.

Mami sets down a glass of water in front of me, and I pretend not to notice her shaking hand. A sharp pop of gunfire explodes outside, making us all jump.

"What are they doing?" Pepito asks.

Mami lets out a long sigh. "They're celebrating, nene."

Pepito scrunches up his face. "That doesn't sound like celebrating to me. There isn't any music."

Eventually they will have music. Of course they will have music. And parades. And speeches. So many speeches. That's what they always do.

But there are always guns first.

More pops of gunfire burst outside. We hear a whizz and snap as a bullet hits the concrete wall of Tía Carmen's house. Pepito, Manuelito, and I instinctively duck our heads, and Mami shouts a word she's smacked me on the back of the head before for saying. Laughter erupts outside along with shouts of "¡Patria o muerte!"

Manuelito, Pepito, and I try to line up the dominoes again, but our hands shake too hard. The tiles keep falling over prematurely. Manuelito gives up and starts gnawing on his fingernails.

A sharp knock interrupts our game, and Tía Carmen opens the door. A man in green fatigues stands in the doorway. His black, greasy beard glistens in the candlelight coming from the kitchen.

"Good evening, compañera. Wonderful evening

for the revolution, no?" he sneers, looking Tía Carmen up and down.

She crosses her arms in front of her. "What do you want?"

The soldier raises his eyebrow. "You hear we defeated the Yanquis?"

"Everyone's heard your nonsense." Tía Carmen clicks her tongue and stares hard at the soldier.

From the kitchen, Mami hisses, "¡Carmencita! ¡Tranquila!"

The soldier pushes past Tía Carmen, the rifle slung over his shoulder smacking against the doorframe. He stands over us sitting at the kitchen table with our dominoes. My palms start to sweat and stick to the plastic tablecloth.

"You boys should be proud. You have witnessed the power of the revolution over the Yanquis. The power of Cuba over the imperialists," he declares, hands on his hips.

Tía Carmen rolls her eyes, and Mami elbows her hard in the ribs.

The soldier turns on his heels and stands an inch from Mami. "You know, compañera, the revolution is always seeking young men for the cause of freedom."

Mami grips the kitchen towel in her hands until I think her knuckles will burst through her skin. I crane my neck to see her face, but the thick stock of the soldier's rifle is in the way. My heartbeat pounds in my ears, making it nearly impossible to hear what he is saying.

"Do you need anything, compañero?" Mami asks, clearing her throat. I know she's trying to distract the soldier from his current line of thought. In the last few weeks, rumors have grown about boys my age and older being shipped off to the Soviet Union to train for the military. Last week, Ladislao Pérez quit coming to school, and Pepito swears he's on a boat headed straight for Moscow. I might think that wasn't true if it weren't for the soldiers' hungry eyes sizing me up every time I walk past the garrison.

The soldier runs his hand through his inky beard. "A glass of water. It's hard work celebrating our victory."

The soldier winks at Mami, and my stomach churns.

Mami fills a glass and hands it to him so quickly water sloshes out onto the tile floor.

The soldier takes a long drink, water droplets sitting in the curls of his coarse beard. He saunters over to our table. "You need a fourth," he says, picking up a tile. The soldier slams his glass onto the table and sets his rifle against the empty chair. The black barrel points at an angle toward Pepito. I grip the table hard, staring at Mami.

She hurries over to us and places both hands on Pepito's shoulders. "They were just about to go to bed," she says, her voice fluttering.

The soldier flips a tile between his fingers and looks at me with black eyes. "And how old are you?"

I swallow hard, almost forgetting my age. "Twelve," I manage.

The soldier places his hand on top of my head and ruffles my hair. His hand is heavy and hot. Mami's grip on Pepito's shoulders tightens.

A sneer grows across the soldier's face. "I imagine we'll be seeing you at the garrison soon. All the sons of Cuba must do their part."

Hot liquid rises in my throat. I think I might throw up.

The shouts increase outside, and the soldier tosses the tile onto the table. He slings his rifle back over his shoulder. Brushing past Tía Carmen and Mami, he exits into the night with a raised fist and a shout of "¡Venceremos!"

I pick up the soldier's discarded tile and flip it over in my hand. Eighteen dots stare up at me like a spray of bullet holes.

The dead man's box.

CHAPTER 2

"If your mami sees that cat, she'll string you up by your toes and dangle you over a pit of crocodiles. You know that, right?"

My friend Serapio punches me in the arm and winks. He shoves another ajonjoli into his mouth, the sesame seeds and sugar leaving a sticky trail at the corner of his lips.

The brown tabby cat purrs and rubs against the leg of my black pants, making me trip on the dirt road as Serapio and I walk home from school. It jumped out as we passed the post office and followed us, hoping Serapio would drop some of his sesame candy.

"Oye, Cumbito," Serapio says. "I've got a winner for AFDF."

I'm not really in the mood to play our usual game of Antes de Fidel, Después de Fidel, where we try to top each other with the most ridiculous ways our lives have changed from before Fidel to after Fidel. I rub my thumb over the domino tile in the pocket of my pants. I've kept the dead man's box tile with me ever since the soldier tossed it onto the table in Tía Carmen's kitchen last week. We returned to our house the next day, Papi emerging from the back bedroom, dark circles under his eyes revealing his long night of sleeplessness and worry. The tile pressed into my leg as my arms cramped from hugging Papi tighter and tighter, fearing he'd disappear if I let go. Since then, Mami and Papi have tried to act like everything is normal, but each time I close my eyes, I feel the soldier's heavy hand on my head and his snarling voice inviting me to the garrison.

"Mira, it's the best," Serapio continues. "So, before Fidel, we had regular chickens."

He pauses and raises his eyebrow at me, expecting me to say something.

"And what do we have after Fidel?" I humor him and ask.

Serapio grins. "After Fidel, we have socialist chickens. They poop in everyone's yard equally."

Serapio's laugh bounces off the stone wall we're walking past, and I groan. I don't offer my submission to Serapio's game because all I can think of is that before Fidel, my family wasn't hiding in fear.

After Fidel, I jump every time I hear the stomp of a soldier's boot on the street.

"Oye, Cumbito. I'm telling you. That cat has mal de ojo. Your mother is going to lose her mind," Serapio mumbles as bits of candy fly from his mouth.

He tries to shoo the cat away, but his hands are covered with sticky sugar syrup from the ajonjoli. He only succeeds in getting brown fur stuck to his fingers.

I shrug. "Doesn't matter if this cat has the evil eye. It could hold an allegiance rally to Mami with all the animals in Cuba and she'd still run screaming for the hills."

"I've never met anyone as scared of animals as your mami."

"Tell me about it. She almost burned the house down that one time Pepito brought three lizards home."

The cat darts behind my legs as a cluster of scowling soldiers shoves six men toward the garrison with their rifles. Yellow shirts hang from the prisoners' slumped shoulders as they shuffle in a line, faces downcast and arms tied behind their backs.

I grab Serapio's arm. "Wait. They're marching more prisoners."

Serapio scans the faces of the men, his fists

clenched and his face white. "You don't think my dad . . . ?"

He swallows hard instead of finishing his sentence.

I shake my head. "No. I don't see him."

Ever since the failed Bay of Pigs invasion a week ago, the government has been rounding up the exiles who fought and anyone else who helped them. A whisper from the Committee for the Defense of the Revolution and you land yourself a yellow shirt and spot in jail.

Serapio's dad was one of the invaders.

We continue down the street, avoiding the prisoners. We pass a tall stone wall, dented and marked with bullet holes. I don't think about what was between the guns and the wall.

The cat abandons its ajonjoli mission and makes a new mission to rub as much fur on my pant leg as it possibly can. I can feel Mami's smack on the back of my head already.

I turn the corner at my street, hoping the cat will continue with Serapio toward his home, but it sticks with me. I pause a block from my house and try to brush off as much of the cat hair from my pants as I can. The cat looks at me with amusement. It heads over to a wall where the Committee for the

Defense of the Revolution has glued up new posters. ¡HASTA LA VICTORIA, SIEMPRE! scream large letters over the image of a bearded man in green fatigues and a beret. The cat stretches upward and drags its claws along the bottom row of posters, tearing one down the middle.

I'm starting to like this cat. HASTA LOS GATOS, SIEMPRE, if you ask me.

I go in the side gate and through the backyard to our kitchen. We never enter through the front of our house because that's where Mami runs her dental practice. The front room of our house is filled with a dentist chair, a desk, and all of Mami's tools. We know not to disturb anything.

And definitely not to let any animals in.

When I enter the kitchen, our maid, Aracelia, is singing at the kitchen sink, her dark curls bouncing along with her hips. Pepito sits at the table behind her, sneaking galletas from a plate on the table. I understand now why he didn't wait for me after school and rushed home before I could catch him. He remembered today was Aracelia's usual day to make cookies.

I brush my hand along the corners of my mouth to show Pepito he has evidence he needs to get rid of. He winks and reaches for another cookie.

Aracelia turns from the sink. "¡Ay, niño! What are you thinking?" she exclaims, waving her hands.

Thinking she's caught Pepito the Cookie Thief, I laugh. Then I feel a warm body brush against my leg.

The cat followed me into the kitchen.

"Por Dios, get that thing out of here right now! Did you mail your brain to the United States?"

Aracelia waves a dish towel at the cat, but it bats its brown paws at the dangling cloth.

I pick up the cat, tossing it outside. It gives me a dirty look, then saunters down the street.

Turning back to the kitchen, I spot Pepito nabbing another cookie. "Would it help to say the cat ripped up a poster of Comandante Che?"

Aracelia sighs. "That's all we need. An antirevolutionary cat in the house."

Pepito chuckles, and cookie crumbs spray from his mouth.

Aracelia puts her hands on her hips and lowers her eyes at Pepito. "If I remember correctly, there were ten galletas on this plate. Niños, you're both worse than el cucuy."

I scuff my feet on the floor. In my opinion, there are worse things to be afraid of now than stolen cookies, stray cats, and the boogeyman. The bullet-marked walls and marching prisoners remind me every time I walk to and from school.

Pepito shoves the plate of cookies away when he sees Mami and Papi enter the kitchen. Papi's linen suit hangs on his thin frame. He takes off his hat, running his hand through his slicked-back hair. Papi opens his mouth to greet us but shakes his head and closes his lips. He shuffles down the hall to their bedroom, shoulders hunched and head bowed.

I start to ask Mami what's wrong, but she claps her hands together. "Bueno, niños. How was school?"

Pepito points a finger and looks at me with devilish eyes. "Cumba brought a cat home."

One of these days, I'm going to design a house and put Pepito's room in a hole in the backyard.

"Pepito probably won't need dinner, Mami. He's been stealing cookies from Aracelia."

Mami shakes her head. "Ay, I should sign you both up for the Committee. You're too good at telling on others."

There's no way I'd ever work for the Committee for the Defense of the Revolution. First, their name is completamente ridículo. Second, they're just a bunch of tattletales that spy on their neighbors and report to the government. Buy meat on the black market? The Committee will report you. Listen to antirevolutionary radio La Voz de las Americas? The Committee will report you.

Manuelito would probably jump at the chance. Last week he told Tía Carmen that Mami traded extra sugar rations for Doña Teresa's teeth cleaning.

The sound of Papi's clarinet flows down the hallway from his bedroom, and for a moment, we are all swept up in Brahms's clarinet trio. The sad notes swirl around the kitchen, and the song increases speed. It sounds like a storm rolling in from the ocean.

Papi played in the orchestra when Presidente Batista was still in power. Now there's no more orchestra. No more music. The song Papi plays usually has a piano and cello as well. Now it's only Papi.

I wander down the hallway, past pictures of Mami and Papi on their wedding day, Pepito as a chubby baby, and me as a skinny baby.

I open the door to Mami and Papi's room and see Papi sitting on the bed. Standing in the doorway, I watch him play. With each breath, his shoulders rise and he sways the clarinet from side to side. At the last note, he lifts the end of the instrument in the air, filling the room with sound. Finishing the song, he lowers the clarinet to his thigh and sits in silence.

"That was good, Papi," I offer.

Startled, he turns and looks at me. I notice tears at the corners of his dark eyes. "Gracias, niño."

He pats the bed, and I move to sit next to him, putting my head on his shoulder. He wraps his arm around me and envelops me in the smell of tobacco and oaky cologne. We watch the tocororo jump from branch to branch on the mango tree outside the bedroom window. Its red, blue, and white feathers match the colors of the Cuban flag. It hops to the ground to pick at a fallen mango.

A scream from the kitchen breaks our silence, and the tocororo flies away.

"¡Ay! ¡Me está mirando!"

The cat must've wandered back into the house. And now Mami is screaming because it's looking at her.

I get up to save Mami from the feline apocalypse, but Papi puts his hand on my shoulder.

"Niño, 'pérate," he says.

I sit back down on the bed. Papi reaches into his pocket and takes out a piece of paper. It's been folded and unfolded so many times it's about to fall apart at the creases.

Papi hands me the paper, and I begin to read.

All sons and daughters of Cuba must do their duty for

the glorious revolution . . . Pioneers against imperialism must train . . . Military service is required of Cuba's children . . .

My heart pounds in my throat, and black spots float in my eyes, keeping me from reading further.

Papi lowers his head and mutters, "They say they're sending children to the Soviet Union for military training."

The hot breeze from the open window sticks to my skin, and my chest heaves, trying to catch a breath.

Swallowing hard, I look at my dad. "Papi, no quiero ir. ¡No quiero ir!"

Papi grabs my hand and squeezes it. "Don't worry. You aren't going. I will not sacrifice my son to Fidel."

He clears his throat and stares out the window. "You're going to the United States."

CHAPTER 3

When Fidel came down from the mountains, the birds flew away. And along with them went President Batista.

Now, instead of birds, we have whispers. Whispers about the government. Whispers about neighbors. They swirl through the air and tickle up your spine. Abuelo whispers that Fidel Castro and Che Guevara aren't heroes for kicking out Cuba's last corrupt president two years ago. Mami whispers that the tanks Fidel rolled down the streets of Havana in victory have now turned against the Cuban people. Neighbors whisper that anyone who flees the island under Fidel's heavy fist is a gusano. A worm and a cobarde.

If I leave, will that make me a coward, too?

My teacher, Padre Tomás, clears his throat and snaps me from my thoughts. "As you can see, estudiantes, when the government owns all the farmland, it can make sure all resources are shared equally."

Padre Tomás rolls his eyes as he says this. His thick black glasses magnify his eyeballs. It's like watching a frog spot a fly on the ceiling. The Cuban government mandates what Padre Tomás can teach, even in a Catholic school, so we've suffered through lectures about agrarian reform and the dangers of foreign influence.

Serapio taps my shoulder and points to the platform at the front of the classroom where Padre Tomás's desk is perched.

"Oye, Cumbito. Today's the day. I can feel it," he says, his brown eyes sparkling with mischief.

Each day before school, Serapio slides Padre Tomás's desk closer to the edge of the platform. Today the front legs of the desk hang an inch over the platform. One good push on a drawer and the desk will topple off the platform and crash to the floor.

My friend Geraldo sits in front of me, and I nudge him in the back. "Get ready, Geraldito. It's gonna happen today."

Geraldo shrugs and reaches into his desk. When Padre Tomás turns toward the chalkboard, Geraldo pulls out a bocadito and takes a bite, bread crumbs and bits of ham falling onto his black uniform pants.

"Oye, Amarito," I whisper to my friend next to me. "Wait for it."

Amaro ignores me. He tries to balance a pencil on his nose but pokes himself in the eye with the tip.

Padre Tomás faces us again, his blond hair slowly fading from the top of his forehead, retreating from the fifteen mischievous sixth-grade boys who torture him daily. Well, maybe not all fifteen of us. Mostly just Serapio.

"Bueno, estudiantes. Do you have any questions over our review of the government's new agricultural measures?" Padre Tomás asks.

Serapio's hand shoots up in the air. The smirk on his face grows.

Ay Dios mío, here we go.

Serapio stands next to his desk and clears his throat. "Padre Bobo, is it true the government is sending students to the countryside to teach? ¿Qué demonios es eso?"

Geraldo chuckles and nearly chokes on his bocadito. Amaro and I have to cover our mouths to keep from laughing.

We found out the first week of school that our Canadian teacher learned Spanish through the Catholic Church. This means he never learned any of those interesting words that usually earn us cocotazos on the back of the head from our mothers. Serapio takes advantage of this and seasons his questions and answers with choice words.

"That's true, Serapio. The government is sending Los Jóvenes Rebeldes to smaller towns in the country."

I look at Amaro. He already knows the answer to Serapio's question. His older brother, Eugenio, was sent by the Young Rebels to a small town near Camagüey to teach patriotismo. But Amaro ignores the conversation and tries to touch his tongue to his nose.

Padre Tomás shuffles over to his desk and opens the top drawer. Serapio and I lean in, our hands clenching our desks in anticipation. Padre Tomás takes out some blank cards from his desk. "These cards are for the Committee for the Defense of the Revolution," he says, holding them up for the class to see.

Padre Tomás's hand rests on the drawer. Serapio and I clench our desks tighter, waiting for him to close it. Instead, he takes off his glasses and rubs his eyes. "Actually, jóvenes," Padre Tomás says, his voice cracking, "I'm supposed to tell you to write down anything you see that would be considered against the Cuban government's new goals. But I just don't think—"

Padre Tomás shuts the drawer of his desk. It's just enough force to send the desk toppling over the platform. It crashes to the floor of our classroom with a thunderous bang. Fifteen boys jump back.

Shouts and laughter fill the classroom. Serapio stands next to his desk again and takes a bow.

I clap for my crazy friend but look at the front of the classroom, where Padre Tomás is standing above his damaged desk. The cards in his hand flutter to the floor, and he once again removes his glasses to rub his eyes.

The school bell rings, declaring the end of the day and saving Padre Tomás from further humiliation. And, more important, saving Serapio from punishment. We tumble out of the classroom, a hurricane of cackles and slaps on the back.

I head to the school courtyard to meet up with Pepito before we walk home.

"Your papi get tired of hiding?" a voice snarls behind me.

I turn and see Manuelito leaning against a column, his eyes narrowed and a scowl growing across his face.

"He probably looks good in yellow shirts, doesn't he?"

I march over to him, stopping an inch from his face. Manuelito may be only a year younger than I am, but I'm about half a foot taller.

"At least my dad still lives on the island," I hiss, looking down on him.

Manuelito opens his mouth to say something, but no sound comes out. "But . . . but," he finally stammers.

I jab my finger into his chest. "Quit talking tontería about my dad. It's not *his* fault your dad left for the United States. And it's not *my* fault your dad didn't return."

Manuelito's cheeks turn red, tears welling up in his eyes. I take a step back. I know I've said too much, but Manuelito picked the wrong day to mess with me.

Shoving my hands into my pockets, I feel the ever-present bumps of the caja de muertos domino. I turn away from Manuelito and walk across the courtyard, spotting Pepito at the entrance gate.

"¿Cómo anda, Cumbito?" Pepito asks.

I pat him on the back. "Well, Serapito finally got Padre Tomás's desk to nose-dive off the platform. He'd been moving it for two weeks."

Pepito laughs. "Ay, poor Padre Tomás. What a going-away present."

I look at Pepito. "Going away? What do you mean?"

"Padre Francisco told us that Fidel is kicking out all the yuma priests. Any priest from another country has to leave," Pepito explains.

On the scale of sins, I wonder how high torturing a priest ranks. Is it worse than letting a friend forget his troubles by amusing himself? Amaro, Geraldo, and I have indulged Serapio's mischief ever since his father disappeared before the Bay of Pigs invasion. Serapio said he thought his dad went to Florida, but his abuela hadn't heard anything.

"Oye, Cumbito," Pepito says, kicking a pebble down the street. "I thought of a good one for AFDF."

I roll my eyes. Pepito always wants to play with us.

"Okay, so before Fidel, I could buy American magazines with cowboys and movie stars," Pepito says, his voice lowered to a whisper so nosy neighbors can't hear.

"I know," I tell him. "What do you think is plastered all over the walls on your side of our room?"

Pepito smiles. "Right. But after Fidel, all we have are Russian magazines in Spanish that tell you everything you never wanted to know about sugarcane farms. This is easily the worst."

I can't help but chuckle. Of all the injustices Fidel and his government have imposed on us, of course Pepito thinks his lack of access to American cowboys is the cruelest of all.

Pepito and I head toward home. We pass Doña Teresa's house, and out jumps a familiar brown tabby cat.

"¡Demonio!" Pepito shouts, crouching down and petting the cat.

"You named the cat 'Demon'?" I ask.

Pepito raises an eyebrow and smiles as the cat purrs against his leg. "Don't you think Mami would agree?"

I put my hands on my hips. "With the name? Yes. With the cat? No way. We'd better lose it before we get home."

"It's not my fault he keeps coming around," Pepito says as we continue our walk home. Despite my attempts to shoo him away, Demonio weaves between our legs.

We pass Parque Vidal in the center of town. Pepito reaches into his pocket and pulls out a piece of crema de leche. He drops it to the ground, and Demonio snaps it up, licking his lips.

I sigh. "Any chance this cat keeps coming around because you keep feeding him candy?"

Pepito smirks and crosses his chest with his finger. "I'm a saint, mal rayo me parta."

I laugh and shake my head. Pepito is always swearing upon penalty of lightning strike. I think of Padre Tomás. If anyone deserves to be struck by lightning, it's probably me.

Maybe I could stand right next to Fidel.

"Mira, Pepito. This cat can't follow us home again. Mami's got too much on her mind lately."

Pepito looks down. "Because you're leaving?"

I start to correct Pepito, to tell him he shouldn't talk about that because the whispers might snatch it up. And talking about it makes something real that so far has only existed in the foggy gray swirl of my dreams.

But a figure crossing the road in front of us catches my eye. Led by soldiers on either side, the man straightens his shoulders and keeps step with his escorts. It isn't until he adjusts his hat that I see who the man is.

Papi.

I stumble, and my hand hits a bullet-marked wall to regain my balance. We thought that Papi was safe after the Bay of Pigs. The government seemed not to care that he went back to being a regular lawyer, which he did after his military service for Batista.

But did they change their minds? What were they doing with Papi?

I grab Pepito's arm and pull him down the street behind Papi and the soldiers. We stay far enough away that I can still see Papi's fists clench as the soldiers at his sides grip the straps of the rifles slung over their shoulders.

It's only when they turn the corner near the post office that I realize where they're headed.

After Fidel took power, Mami and Papi told me and Pepito to never go near the prison in Santa Clara. The small, one-story building with a walled courtyard seemed innocent enough, but Fidel was filling it with anyone he thought opposed the revolution.

Had the whispers finally reached Papi? Had they slithered around his wrists like shackles?

"Cumba, where are we going?" Pepito whines, dragging his feet. I don't want to tell him who we're following because I don't want him to be as scared as I am.

The soldiers push Papi into the prison courtyard and slam a heavy metal gate behind them, the sharp sound echoing down the street.

Pepito yanks his hand from mine, his eyes darting across the walls of the prison. "We're not supposed to be here. Mami and Papi said. What are you doing?"

I swallow hard and try to make my voice as calm as possible. "I need to see something. Don't worry."

I pull Pepito over to a tall jaguey tree looming over the wall surrounding the prison courtyard, and he crouches between the large, drooping roots, a scowl on his face. I scramble up the tree and perch myself in its branches, just above the wall but hidden from the soldiers in the courtyard.

Papi stands with one soldier. A few others smoke cigars and laugh as they load their rifles.

Two soldiers emerge from inside the prison, dragging a man about Abuelo's age between them. His crumpled clothes are marked with dirt. I search his face, the wrinkles that spread from his dark eyes, his lips pulled in a tight line, to see if I recognize him. But I don't. He's just another person who made Fidel angry.

My fingers dig into the bark of the jaguey tree as the soldiers shove the old man to a bare wall of the prison.

The soldier next to Papi sneers and says, "Compañero Fernandez, we are so grateful to have a lawyer of your fine standing in our town."

The soldier sounds anything but thankful, and the smirk plastered on his face reveals his sarcasm.

"Your presence here today for these proceedings will confirm that the revolution is fair and just." The soldier's lip curls into a snarl under the curly black hair of his beard.

I watch as Papi holds his hat in his hand, his knuckles about to tear the cream fabric in two. He opens his mouth to speak, but the old man gives Papi the slightest nod. Papi's shoulders sag, and he mumbles something to the soldier that I can't make out.

My eyes lock on Papi as the soldiers finish loading their rifles. I notice tears glistening in the corners of his eyes as the sun looms lower on the horizon.

I want to run to Papi and pull him away from the courtyard. I want to take the old man with us and hide him in our house.

A line of rifles forms in front of the old man, and my stomach rolls. Pepito kicks the dirt below me, and I hear him start to scramble up the tree.

"Don't come up here," I tell him, unable to hide the edge in my voice. "Stay down there. Just stay down there."

That's when the singing starts.

The old man stands against the wall, his shoulders square and his chest puffed out as he sings "La Bayamesa," the Cuban national anthem. The notes float over the soldiers, across the courtyard, and rustle the leaves of the jaguey tree.

Do not fear a glorious death.

The soldier next to Papi shouts, and the firing squad readies their rifles.

For to die for the homeland is to live.

Another shout and the soldiers aim their rifles. Pepito's hand grabs my ankle as he climbs up the tree.

To live in chains is to live
Mired in shame and disgrace.

One final shout and a series of cracks puncture the air. The singing stops. Pepito's eyes grow wide, and his mouth drops open as he peeks over the wall.

"No!" I yell, pushing him away from the sight. We lose our grips and tumble from the tree, landing in a tangle of limbs with a hard thud in the dirt.

The leaves of the jaguey tree hang still, no longer rustled by the old man's song. The prison gate creaks, and heavy footsteps scuff in the dirt away from us.

Pepito trembles in my arms as his tears soak my shirt.

"I want to go home," he whimpers.

I keep my arm tight around his shoulders, making sure to put myself between Pepito and the prison. Legs shaking, we make our way back down the street, toward our house.

As the soldiers behind us in the prison begin shouting at one another, I can't help but wonder who will take care of Pepito after I fly away.

CHAPTER 4

I bite into my breakfast of bread with thick slices of guava, the sticky sweetness doing little to calm the storm in my stomach. Red globs of guava fall onto the tablecloth, looking too much like the aftermath of the rifle fire at the prison.

I swallow hard, hoping to keep down my breakfast—and my fear.

Mami and Papi talked in hushed whispers about the execution he was forced to watch. I heard him tell Mami that he thought it was the government's way of punishing him. Pepito and I didn't tell them we were there. We would've been banned from ever leaving the house again.

Pepito's coughs echo throughout the kitchen.

"Ay, Mami, I'm dying," Pepito spits out in a hoarse voice. He looks miserable, as if some unknown virus has him on the verge of death and his corpse will be researched by scientists.

His tapping foot under the table betrays his nervousness and true motives.

The night after the execution at the prison, I heard Pepito's muffled sobs across our bedroom as he pressed his face into his pillow. He crawled into bed with me, and we slept back to back, his trembling body trying to forget what he saw. He's slept in my bed for the past five nights.

Pepito doesn't want to go outside. He fears the soldiers marching down the street and the rifles they carry slung over their shoulders. He fears his neighbors, who one minute share a café con leche with you and the next minute whisper to the government about what you've been doing.

This fear is his true virus. It's mine as well.

"Niño, you're not dying," my abuela says, patting Pepito on the head. She sits with him and strokes his head, her wrinkled fingers running through his brown hair. Abuela hums a song about elephants bouncing on a spider thread, and Pepito nestles into her shoulder.

"Dale agua," Mami says to Abuela. "He needs to drink water."

Mami's solution for everything is a glass of water. Fever? Agua. Stomachache? Agua. Decapitation? Agua.

Abuela pulls out a bar of chocolate from her blue housedress instead.

Pepito starts to smile but looks at Mami and then groans, clutching his stomach.

Mami raises an eyebrow at her mother-in-law and shakes her head. She sighs and turns to me. "You are ready to go, no?"

I take one last bite of my bread and gulp down the last bit of café con leche from the bottom of my cup. "Sí, Mami."

Mami says we have an important errand today. She's even taken the day off from her dental practice to do it. I don't know where we're going, but Mami has never canceled on her patients. Luckily, we live next door to Papi's parents, so Abuela can stay with Pepito while we're gone.

Mami and I head for the door, and I feel chubby arms wrap around my waist. Pepito releases me and looks up with searching eyes.

"Be careful," he pleads.

I pat him on the head. "No te preocupes, hermanito. Don't worry. I'll be fine."

Pepito sits back down next to Abuela and pushes the chocolate bar across the table away from him. Abuela wraps her arms around him and brushes his hair off his sweaty forehead.

Mami and I leave and begin our walk to her top secret errand.

"What was that all about?" she asks as we turn the corner at the end of the street.

"Nada," I reassure her. "Pepito's been making up stories about fire-breathing dragons he thinks live in our neighborhood."

I puff out my chest, proud of myself for making up an excuse so quickly, but my eyes dart down each street, not expecting dragons but soldiers. My ears strain for marching boots.

Pepito isn't the only one who's had trouble sleeping.

"Where are we going?" I ask Mami.

She clenches her purse and stares straight ahead. Her short, quick steps echo against the concrete houses.

"You need a new suit before you leave," she says. The last word catches in her throat, and she swallows. Her hand begins to rub the small gold cross hanging from her neck.

I look down and fumble with the sleeves of my shirt, pulling them over my wrists.

We pass a newsstand with papers blaring that Fidel has canceled elections. ELECTIONS? WHY? THE PEOPLE HAVE ALREADY CHOSEN, the headline reads.

Fidel doesn't want to know if we've changed our minds.

El sastre, the tailor, is just past the newsstand. We enter the small shop crammed with every color of guayabera imaginable. The intricately embroidered button-down shirts are the unofficial uniform of Cuban men. I wonder if Mami will let me pick one out or if I'll be stuck with a traditional suit.

El sastre comes out from behind a thick green curtain covering the doorway at the back of the shop.

"Buenos días, Señora Fernandez," he says, taking Mami's hand in his own.

"Good day, Señor Schneider," Mami responds, stumbling over el sastre's last name. It comes out more like "Nider" since most of us in Santa Clara have trouble pronouncing our German tailor's name.

El sastre looks me up and down. "My, but you are growing so quickly. Like a weed, no?"

"I'm almost as tall as my papi," I tell him, my fingers picking at the buttons on my shirt.

He shuffles over to a drawer and pulls out a measuring tape. He motions for me to stand on a small platform in front of a dusty mirror.

His age-spotted hands trail the measuring tape

along my shoulders, his rolled-up sleeves revealing a tattoo on his forearm. El sastre catches me looking at the blurred blue numbers.

"From another time," he says, looking at me with watery green eyes over his glasses.

He writes down my measurements in a small notebook. El sastre looks past Mami and into the street outside his shop.

"I suppose we have one more item of business. Correct, señora?"

I wonder if I'm getting a guayabera along with my suit.

El sastre moves to the back of his shop and motions us behind the curtain that divides the front of the store from the back. I shoot Mami a puzzled look but follow her.

Mami pulls some papers out of her purse and hands them to el sastre.

"Will his photo on this work?" she asks.

El sastre takes the papers and heads to a small desk. He removes a pair of tweezers from a drawer and unfolds the papers.

They're my government identification papers. What is going on?

El sastre presses the tweezers under my photo and lifts it from my identification papers. He takes a small blue notebook out from another drawer in the desk and opens it to the first page.

It's not a notebook. It's a passport.

"Mami?"

"To leave, the government says you have to have a passport and a letter that says you're going abroad to expand your studies. But they aren't exactly passing them out these days. El sastre knows how to do this."

El sastre smiles. "This isn't the first one of these I've done, you know. Many a passport in Germany bears the mark of Johan Schneider."

I scrunch my eyebrows together, and el sastre smiles. "Much like Castro, Herr Hitler wanted certain people to 'vanish,' shall we say. Those who needed to escape needed the proper identification. Or, at least, they needed identification that looked proper, just like you."

He takes glue, brushes it on the back of my photo, and presses the photo onto the first page of the passport. El sastre shuffles over to me with stooped shoulders and pats me on the head.

"I think you are too old, no?"

"One year will be enough," Mami says. She's wrung her hands on her purse so much a seam starts to rip at the top.

I look at Mami. She brushes a thin line of sweat from her forehead. A perfect brown curl presses against her temple. "You are too close to the correct age for the Young Rebels. They'll turn you away at the airport and send you straight to the garrison. Your papi and I don't want you to be controlled by the government. We don't want you to join the military. We need to make you just a little younger."

I want to respond, but my mouth is filled with sand. I can see the soldier's hard face and the glint of his rifle as I hand him a fake passport at the airport.

As if sensing my doubt, el sastre places his hand on my shoulder. "Young man, it will be fine. You look them right in the eye when you hand them this. Always look them right in the eye."

I nod.

El sastre begins filling out my passport with a black fountain pen. I notice he changes my birth date to December 27, 1949. Just like that, Manuelito and I are the same age.

El sastre looks at Mami. "Now remember, señora, if you need the same, I can do it."

My head snaps toward Mami. "Are you going, too?"

Mami shakes her head and gives me a tight smile. "No, niño. The government isn't letting out any medical professionals. Even dentists. Lawyers can't leave, either. Your father and I would never make it past the airport. It's more important that you leave. We can't risk your having to join the Young Rebels. You know that's just one step away from the military."

I slump my shoulders. My hope of not having to do this alone vanishes like a blown-out candle.

I shift my gaze to the pictures hanging in el sastre's back room, trying to distract my racing thoughts and nerves. I land on a photograph of a woman and young girl, bundled in coats and standing in snow. The white powder reaches up to their shins, and the young girl is hanging on to her mother's arm, laughing. I wonder what it would be like to feel snow, to be so cold that you cling to someone else for warmth.

"You know," el sastre says, snapping me from my trance, "I know a little about leaving your home country behind."

"When did you come to Cuba?" I ask.

"Nineteen forty-one. I was one of the few that made it off a ship that your country turned away. America, too. Those of us trying to escape aren't always wanted. Remember that."

I wipe my sweaty palms on my pants. "Does your family miss the snow?"

El sastre reaches up and caresses the faces of the woman and child under the glass frame.

"No, no, I don't imagine they do. They are buried under the snow," he says, hands shaking over the photo. "I came to Cuba alone."

El sastre stamps my passport with an official number and seal and gives it to me. It burns in my hands.

This is real. Going to the United States is now real.

I look at Mami. I want to grab her hand and bury myself in the small red flowers on her dress. She gives me a weak smile as she takes the passport from me, depositing it in her purse.

"Oye, polaco," a sharp voice calls from the front of the store.

El sastre places his finger to his lips with one hand and motions for us to stay put with the other.

"Buenos días, compañero," el sastre says as he goes to the front of the shop. Mami and I press ourselves against the wall so as not to be seen when he opens the curtain.

"You're not gonna be in business much longer, are you, polaco?"

I know that voice. It's the voice of the soldier who burst into Tía Carmen's house. My palms start to sweat again, and the caja de muertos domino in my pocket gains ten pounds.

"Soon the Federation of Cuban Women will be running this store. It will belong to the people."

Mami grabs my hand. I'm certain the soldier can hear my heart slamming in my chest. My shirt feels sticky against my back as Mami and I press ourselves against the wall.

I hear el sastre clear his throat. "Until then, you are here for your wife's dress, are you not?"

El sastre's arm reaches behind the curtain, and I see him pull a plastic package containing a light beige dress off a shelf.

There's more shuffling on the other side of the curtain, and I hear el sastre say, "Can I interest you in a guayabera? You must need a break from wearing green all the time, no? Such a boring color."

A deep chuckle comes from the soldier, but it doesn't sound like he's smiling.

"We'll see, polaco. We'll see." Coins drop on the counter with a sharp clank.

Heavy footsteps fade as the soldier leaves the shop.

I let out the hot breath I held for their entire conversation.

El sastre returns to the back of the shop. He gives Mami and me a reassuring nod.

"Why'd he call you *polaco*? You're from Germany, not Poland," I ask.

"The less educated of your citizens assume all Jews are from Poland. Perhaps Fidel does need to improve the schools." He looks at me and winks.

El sastre reaches for Mami's hand. "I believe that is all our business today. His suit and his letter from the Ministry of Education should be ready next week."

"Muchas gracias, señor. We appreciate your work," she replies.

He once again places a wrinkled hand on my shoulder. Leaning down and looking me in the eye, he says, "Young man. You never really leave. You never really escape."

El sastre's voice catches, and he takes off his glasses.

"Your heart will always be in Cuba."

CHAPTER 5

Abuelo once told me that Cuba was created from God's tears because he had to leave his creation. Padre Tomás said the island was formed by volcanoes and tectonic plate shift.

Hiking the hills outside Santa Clara, I decide it's both. The trees drip with humidity, God's tears falling from the leaves. Stand still long enough and you can feel the island tremble, quivering with unrest.

Abuelo, Papi, Pepito, and I walk past the rows of buildings in town, the tobacco and sugarcane farms on the outskirts, and into the hills outside Santa Clara. Small creeks snake their way through the hills, meandering and searching for a way to the ocean. Royal palms stand guard over our path, reaching up to the sky like rockets, exploding in green leaves at the top.

When I was little, before Pepito was born, Abuelo

used to show me how he could climb to the top of one, while Abuela stood below muttering a prayer over and over.

"Ay Dios mío, that man is going to give me a heart attack. Then we'll see who will make his food and clean his house," she'd say, wagging her finger at him far above.

"Doesn't Aracelia do that?" I'd ask, reminding Abuela of the maid they shared with us.

As always, Abuela would cement her hands to her hips. "Cállate, nene."

Today Papi is hunting for a black orchid to give to Mami. Royal palms and banyan trees fill the hills outside Santa Clara, while white jasmine and hibiscus grow lazily underneath. But Papi is looking for a very specific purple-and-yellow blossom. It's Mami's favorite.

"Zunzuncito? Where are you, zunzuncito?" Pepito calls.

He trots down the path searching for a bee hummingbird. The red-and-white bird is the smallest hummingbird in the world, according to Padre Tomás. I think they're just mutant mosquitoes.

"Pepito, you're making too much noise. They'll never get near you stomping around like that," I say, scanning our path for Papi's flower.

Abuelo puts his hand on my shoulder. "Let him be. It's good for him to run around."

Abuelo fans himself with his hat. His white guayabera sticks to his back with sweat. His dress pants and shirt aren't ideal for trekking through the hills, but as the former postmaster of Santa Clara, he believes in looking his best and representing his position well.

My pants aren't much better. But only little kids wear shorts, like Pepito. And the way he keeps swatting at the mosquitoes dive-bombing his legs, I don't mind.

Papi scans the sides of the trail, concentrating on the bases of the banyan trees, looking for the elusive black orchid. Pepito trots up and down the trail but never strays too far from his side, even holding on to Papi's hand at times.

He still sleeps in my bed.

Just southwest of Santa Clara, the hills rise steeply, encouraging us to roll right back into town. We reach the crest of the tallest hill, and my lungs threaten mutiny.

"Zunzuncito!" Pepito shouts, pointing to what I'm certain is a mosquito.

He drags Papi by the arm off the trail, Papi's shoulders heaving from the climb up the hill. Abuelo walks over to a tree and reaches up into its branches. He snaps off a pink-and-green oval-shaped fruit.

Holding up the fruit in front of me, he says, "Did you know that mango is God's favorite fruit?"

I arch an eyebrow at Abuelo. "Oh, really? How do you know that?"

Abuelo waves his hand at the surrounding hills. "Because Cuba is God's favorite place, and he filled it with mango."

I chuckle and roll my eyes.

I sit on a rock, and Abuelo joins me. He takes a knife from his pocket and slices a piece of mango, the bright juice dripping down his hand. He pulls out a handkerchief and wipes the sticky orange sweetness from his fingers.

"Mami bought me a new suit last week," I say between bites of mango.

Abuelo smiles. "Sí, your papi told me. Quite an adventure you're going on, no?"

He wipes his mouth with his handkerchief and pats me on the knee. "No te preocupes, chico. You won't be gone long."

I raise my eyebrows at Abuelo. "What?"

"Fidel won't be here for long. He'll fly away just like Batista. The Americans won't let him stay in power."

"But they already tried to get rid of him once, and it didn't work."

Abuelo shrugs. "Maybe, but the Americans are persistent, no? They won't allow someone like Fidel to rule. To them, socialism is a cancer. They won't let it fester just ninety miles away from them."

Abuelo stands and tucks his handkerchief back into his pocket. "You'll be back home in a couple of months. Te lo juro."

A couple of months? I could stand anything for a couple of months. I survived Papi's teaching Pepito to play the violin, the screeching sound of a drowning cat seeping through every corner of our house. I survived Serapio's attempts to convince Padre Tomás that our entire class could speak only German, not Spanish. He made us memorize German flash cards for two months.

I could survive the United States. Maybe it would be an adventure, just like Abuelo promised.

"Vamos, chico. Let's go help your papi," Abuelo says, placing his hat back on his head.

We continue down the trail, the royal palms giving way to more banyan trees. Their large trunks draped with runner roots thicken the vegetation in the hills, choking out the breeze and wrapping us in humidity. Abuelo used to tell me the banyan trees were the ghosts of viudas, old widows with their arms outstretched, tattered and ripped clothing hanging down to the ground.

I can still hear Pepito crashing through the brush, Papi trying to keep up with him.

Down the path, I spot a yellow-and-purple blossom peeking out from under the roots of a banyan tree.

"Papi, I found one!" I shout, running over to the flower.

I crouch down, inspecting the blossom. Purple petals fading to curly yellow tendrils snaking down to the ground.

"You found a good one," a deep voice says from behind the banyan tree.

A thick black boot steps over a banyan root. I look up and see that the boot is attached to a green-fatigued soldier. He chews on a short cigar stub, brown juice dripping from the corners of his mouth and into his curly black beard.

My breath catches in my throat, and I brace my hand against the tree. I don't know if he remembers me, but this is the same soldier who barged into Tía Carmen's house and who harassed el sastre. Even though most soldiers grow dark beards to look just like Fidel, I'd recognize his deep, menacing voice anywhere.

"You lost, joven?" he sneers.

Abuelo rushes to my side and pulls me up from the ground.

"Buenos días," Abuelo says, taking off his hat and placing it over his chest. "Good day for a walk, no?"

Papi and Pepito come back on the trail and stop when they see the soldier. The color drains from Papi's face, and Pepito hides behind him, holding his hand in a death grip.

"Yes, it is a good day," the soldier says. "Fidel has blessed us with many good days. Not like when we had that cobarde Batista."

He trains his black eyes on Papi. "Isn't that right, Ramón?"

Papi's eyebrows pinch together as he inspects the soldier. Then his eyes grow wide.

"Ignacio?"

The soldier takes the cigar from his mouth and rests his hand on the pistol in the holster at his side. "Sí, hombre. Didn't think you'd recognize me."

Papi moves toward the soldier but keeps Pepito firmly behind him.

"This is Ignacio Fuentes. We went to school together," he explains to Abuelo and me.

The soldier sticks out his hand to Abuelo. Sweat

stains trail from under his arms and down his chest like smelly snakes. "Encantado."

Abuelo gives a weak smile but doesn't take the soldier's hand. "Ignacio? Carlos and Lidia's boy?"

I look past Ignacio and notice four more soldiers just down the hill. Their rifle barrels catch the sunlight and pierce my eyes.

"And what are you doing in the hills this fine day?" Ignacio asks, rubbing the black grip of his pistol.

Abuelo takes his handkerchief from his pocket and wipes his forehead. He places his hat back on his head and gives Ignacio a smile. "Bueno, we are looking for a special flower. Do you suppose Fidel would mind if we picked one?"

Ignacio chuckles but keeps his hand on his pistol. "Ay, viejo, I remember you. Not a friend of that cobarde Batista, if I recall."

I grip Abuelo's hand and rub my thumb on the scars that circle his wrist. Abuelo told me long ago that's what happens when shackles are left on too long. Abuelo was thrown into prison for two years by Presidente Batista when he was caught distributing pamphlets that listed the government's crimes against the Cuban people. But now Abuelo grumbles that we traded one dictator for another.

Ignacio looks at Abuelo expectantly, but Abuelo says nothing.

"Although your son was another story," Ignacio says, pointing his cigar at Papi. "Jumped right into that uniform, didn't you, Ramón?"

Papi wipes the sweat from his forehead with the back of his hand. His chest heaves in a sigh. "You know I just wore the uniform. They sent me to law school. That was it. It never meant anything to me."

Ignacio's grip on his pistol tightens, and his knuckles turn white. "I guess we all had our own ways of surviving, didn't we?"

I always wondered how Abuelo felt about Papi's working for Batista. Papi was the first person in our family to go to college, and I know Abuelo and Abuela are proud of him. I never knew that Batista's government paid for it. Maybe this soldier is right; we all have our own ways of surviving.

Papi and Ignacio stare at each other. A mosquito lands on my neck, but I can't make myself move to slap it away. A sting pinches my skin, and I wince.

Abuelo clears his throat. "And what are Fidel's best soldiers doing on this fine day?"

Ignacio narrows his eyes. "Just making sure the woods aren't crawling with gusanos. And if they are . . ." He rubs the grip of his pistol.

I know that for Fidel, gusanos are not only anyone who's against his government, but also homosexuals, disabled people, even priests like Padre Tomás.

Abuelo points to the stripes on Ignacio's fatigues. "You seem to have done well for yourself, young man."

"I only have what always should have been mine. Fidel is redistributing what belongs to all Cubans. We work hard, and we all benefit."

He takes the pistol out of its holster and waves it at the surrounding hills. "We only need to rid the island of this imperialist disease."

Abuelo clears his throat. "Yes, Cuba does belong to all of us. But she doesn't hold us prisoner, does she? She knows her people are like the tocororo. They die in captivity."

Ignacio stares at Abuelo. Papi steps closer to me, putting his hand firmly on my shoulder. Pepito remains hidden behind Papi's back, but I can hear his quick breath.

"And who is this?" Ignacio asks, waving his pistol at me.

I grip Abuelo's arm and try to answer, but I'm afraid I'll throw up if I open my mouth.

"My grandson."

Ignacio rolls his eyes. "And his name?"

I hear a voice break next to me. "Cumba," Papi says.

Ignacio slides the pistol back into its holster. That does little to slow my heart pounding in my chest.

"And how old are you?" he asks.

Abuelo starts to answer, but I know he'll give my real age and not the one on my forged passport.

"Eleven," I lie, squeezing Abuelo's hand. Ignacio already asked me this that night after the Bay of Pigs, but I'm thankful he doesn't seem to remember me or the age I told him.

Ignacio puts the cigar stub back in his mouth and smiles, his dark eyes glistening. "Ay, you could be a Young Rebel."

"But I'm not old enough," I reply without thinking.

"Don't worry," Ignacio sneers. "We always make an exception for true patriots. After all, the son of Ramón Fernandez would make an excellent Young Rebel."

He pulls a green fatigue cap from the pocket of his uniform pants and slaps it onto his head. As he takes a step toward me, Abuelo's grip on my arm tightens.

"Cumba Fernandez, I will see you at the garrison on July tenth."

He looks at Abuelo and then at Papi. "Compañeros, I know you will get him there."

He touches his finger to the brim of his cap. "Good day, familia Fernandez," he says.

Ignacio turns on his heels and marches down the trail to join the other soldiers, stomping the delicate petals of the black orchid with his thick boots.

Papi wraps me in his arms. I bury my face in his chest and try not to cry.

"Estoy bien. Estoy bien. I'm okay. I'm okay," I mumble over and over, thinking my repetition will make it true.

Abuelo puts his hand on my back. "Vamos, chico. Let's go home."

We trod down the hill toward Santa Clara, a somber funeral procession. Pepito says nothing, and I hear him sniffle behind me as we reach the bottom of the hill.

July tenth. July tenth. July tenth.

The date pounds in my mind with each step as the caja de muertos tile slams in my pocket against my leg.

The United States may be an adventure. But I've got to get there first.

CHAPTER 6

My parents have made a deal with Padre Tomás to punish me. They've cooked up some grand plan to make me memorize the Ten Commandments in five languages while balancing a dictionary on my head. I'm certain of it.

That's the only reason I can come up with to explain why they sat me down at the kitchen table before I left for school and in lowered voices told me I had to wait after school in Padre Tomás's classroom and follow his instructions.

I wanted to ask them why, wanted to say I was sorry for being part of the desk-toppling prank, even though I'm not sure how they found out about it. But lately every question I ask seems to be met with dismissal. With a quick "don't worry; it'll be fine."

As the whispers get louder in our neighborhood, and in my own house, the less people tell me.

After class, Serapio tries to pull me out of the classroom, but I shrug him off, making up an excuse about needing help with our latest math assignment.

Once everyone clears out of the classroom, I approach Padre Tomás's desk. He stands behind his chair and takes a deep breath.

"Thank you for staying, Cumba," he says. His eyes look tired behind his glasses. "Did your parents explain everything?"

I shake my head. "No, sir."

"Oh, well, if you would just wait here for a minute, I'll be right back." Padre Tomás disappears into the small room off our classroom that serves as his office.

I look at his desk perched on the platform at the front of the room, the edges scuffed and scratched from the nosedive it took after Serapio's prank. That seems like forever ago, even though it was just three weeks.

Padre Tomás emerges from the room, and my eyes widen. He's dressed in a beige linen suit, a small suitcase gripped in his hand. I've never seen him in anything other than the dark cassock that priests always wear.

"I have to go," he says in a quiet voice. He takes a

deep breath, trying to find words that don't seem to be there.

I search Padre Tomás's face. "What do you mean? Where are you going?"

"Fidel is making all the foreign-born priests leave. He's kicking us out of the country." Padre Tomás picks at the corner of the desk he's standing next to, his fingers trembling. "They say he's going to close all the schools soon. So many of you boys are being sent to the countryside with the Young Rebels, we won't have much of a class anyway."

Padre Tomás is right. Just this week, Pineda Hernandez and Camilo Diaz stopped coming to school, and the whispers said they'd been sent to work in the sugarcane fields with the Young Rebels.

I scuff my feet on the floor as my stomach flip-flops. Fidel gets to decide who stays and who goes. He decides if kids get to stay with their families or work in the countryside. He says what we can buy at the store and what we should say to our neighbors.

What if he thinks it's his choice who lives and who dies?

"What do you need me for?" I ask my teacher.

Padre Tomás sets his suitcase down, takes off his glasses, and rubs his eyes. "Government spies are waiting to see where the priests will go. A family has agreed to take me in since I have nowhere else to stay, but I don't want the spies to follow me and get this family in trouble. I'm going to walk out of here and wander around town for a bit. I need you to leave a few minutes after me with my suitcase and do the same. Go to this address, and drop off my suitcase. That way we can hopefully confuse the spies and keep everyone safe."

Padre Tomás reaches into the pocket of his suit and hands me a small piece of paper. I read the address and swallow hard when I recognize it. This is Geraldo's address.

I nod in agreement. Normally, I would think this was an adventure, like being in a spy novel. But my heartbeat slamming in my ears corrects me. Sometimes stories in books aren't as fun in real life.

I take Padre Tomás's suitcase as he looks around the classroom. His eyes stop on the small crucifix hanging on the wall above the chalkboard. Taking the cross down, he rubs the wooden edges with his thumb. He tucks the crucifix into his jacket pocket, and his eyes scan the desks in our classroom as his shoulders sag. He seems to be memorizing each chair, each squirmy twelve-year-old who sat there.

Is this what it's like to leave? To have to say goodbye?

Clearing his throat, he walks up to me and places a hand on my shoulder.

"Thank you, Cumba. It's been an honor being your teacher. Being a teacher to all you boys."

I nod and smile. "Even Serapio?"

Padre Tomás chuckles, his voice echoing in the empty classroom. "Yes, especially Serapio. I firmly believe God loves rascals best."

I watch as Padre Tomás walks out of the classroom, placing a hat just like Papi owns on his head. He pulls it down to his eyes and walks through the school courtyard, his head lowered.

I wait a few minutes, counting the dots on the caja de muertos in my pocket over and over. I would bite my fingernails, but I've ground each to a stub ever since running into Ignacio in the countryside a week ago. My stomach rolls as I mentally plan my route to Geraldo's house. I know I shouldn't go straight there, like Padre Tomás said. And I shouldn't go the same way he went.

I leave the classroom, suitcase gripped in my sweaty hand, and make my way down the street, away from school. I pass the post office where Abuelo taught me the alphabet by letting me sort mail. I round the corner and pass Tío Enrique and Tía Rosita's house, where Tía Rosita used to give me Coke mixed with sweetened condensed milk because she thought I was too skinny as a baby. I trip on my shoelaces when I pass the movie theater where Pepito and I used to watch American cowboy movies that now plays Russian movies dubbed in Spanish.

It's after the theater that I notice I have a shadow.

A man wearing a blue suit and gray hat follows me when I turn toward Parque Vidal. He grips the folded newspaper in his hand and follows me through the park and down the street toward the prison. He's still at my back when I pass a woman who watches me with narrowed eyes, sizing me up to see if I'm doing anything she should report. I can see him in the reflection of Dr. Álvarez's office window, a large sign behind the glass declaring "Socialism or Death!"

My feet ache, and I have a blister on my heel that burns every time I take a step. I'm five blocks from Geraldo's house. If I can just make it there, I can pass off the suitcase and rest.

My shirt sticks to my back with sweat. I want to run, or even simply walk faster, but I don't want to tip off the man that I'm aware he's following me. For all he knows, I'm an obedient son, carrying a suitcase of tailored clothes from el sastre.

That thought gives me an idea.

I turn on my heels and walk in the opposite direction, directly at the man following me. My heartbeat is racing, but I take a deep breath, trying my best to appear calm.

"¡Ay, que tontería! I forgot my change at el sastre's," I exclaim, smacking my forehead dramatically. Pepito would be proud of my acting skills.

Always look them in the eye.

That's what el sastre said, and that's what I do.

"Buenas tardes, compañero," I say as I pass the man, mustering as much confidence in my voice as I can.

The man nods at me with dark eyes and pursed lips but keeps going. I don't look back as I sharply turn a corner and run down the street as fast as my shaking legs will allow. I turn a corner again, putting even more distance between me and the man, and duck into a doorway. Crouching down and clutching the suitcase to my chest, I catch my breath. I look at the building across the street and find myself inspecting it for good places to hide.

There's an AFDF for you, Serapio, I think. Before Fidel, I'd spend hours walking the streets in Santa Clara and marveling at the beautiful architecture, the stone buildings with decorated columns and scrolls along the roofline. After Fidel, the bullet-scarred buildings are only good for hiding.

I wait and bite the nails my nerves destroyed days ago, my fingertips stinging. I wait and count the dots on the caja de muertos. I wait until I'm certain the man has decided he was following an idiot boy who forgot to collect his change from the tailor when his mami sent him on an errand.

Once I think it's safe, I scurry toward Geraldo's house. His mother greets me at the door with a whisper of "he made it, too," collecting the suitcase and shutting the door again. I want to collapse on her doorstep, but I know Papi and Mami are waiting for me at home.

I weave through the streets of Santa Clara once again, passing large portraits of Fidel and Che plastered in windows. A group of boys not much older than me, dressed in the olive drab clothes of the Young Rebels, spit at my feet and yell "Patria o muerte" as I pass. Fresh bullet holes in walls stare at me as I make my way home.

As the royal palms start to sway in the warm evening breeze, I wonder when my country became a place I hardly recognize anymore.

CHAPTER 7

Padre Tomás was right, as always. Fidel canceled school. Permanently.

The government wanted to make sure the lessons taught in Cuban schools were in line with Fidel's socialist society, scrubbed clean of any religious or capitalist ideas. As if one tainted lesson would turn us into Yanquis singing "The Star-Spangled Banner." So they canceled classes until a review of all schools is completed.

Serapio, Amaro, Geraldo, and I spend our days in Parque Vidal, swapping AFDF stories and daring one another to talk to the girls sitting under the large jaguey trees.

I rub the caja de muertos domino in my pocket, the image of Padre Tomás standing in our classroom with tears in his eyes keeping me from listening as Serapio tells us about his latest scheme to get Juanita to talk to him.

"I'll do my hair just like one of those American

movie stars. Maybe John Wayne or Clark Gable. She won't be able to resist me," Serapio declares as he stands on a park bench, hands on his hips.

Juanita sits on a low stone wall across the park with four other girls, all wearing dresses and flipping their hair when they laugh. If any of them actually do talk to Serapio, he'll probably just throw up at their feet.

"Cuidado, Serapito. You're forgetting AFDF," I warn him. "Before Fidel, you could dress as American as you wanted. After Fidel, you have to wear olive-colored or brown clothes. And grow a beard like Fidel or Che . . . but I don't think you can. Maybe smear shoe polish all over your chin."

I punch him in the thigh, and he jumps down from the bench.

Serapio raises an eyebrow. "Maybe I should start smoking cigars."

I roll my eyes. "You smell bad enough to keep Juanita away. A cigar definitely won't help."

Serapio slaps me on the arm and laughs.

"I'm bored," Geraldo says, kicking a pebble across the park. "Let's go get a Coke."

"Geraldito, how many times do I have to tell you?" Serapio says. "That basura they sell at the store is not Coke. It's some garbage Che cooked up."

When Fidel and Che kicked out all the

foreign-owned business, that included the Coca-Cola bottling company in Havana. Che took over the factory with his own version of Coke. Each sip is a lie. It looks like real Coke but tastes like Demonio used the bottle as a bathroom.

Serapio laughs. "One sip and you turn into a zombie, mumbling socialismo, socialismo."

He extends his arms and shuffles around the park.

"Serapito, deja," I hiss. "The soldiers will see you."

A handful of soldiers patrol the park, smoking cigarettes and making comments to women passing by.

Serapio lowers his arms and claps. "Oye, chicos. Championship AFDF round. What d'you got?"

Geraldo bites his lip and lowers his voice. "Before, my mami could buy meat whenever she wanted. After, the butcher won't let her because he says we listen to imperialist radio."

We all listen to American radio stations using shortwave radios in our houses, even though that's not allowed. I had to slap Serapio the other day when I caught him humming an Elvis Presley song we heard. Not being able to buy meat is an easy punishment. Our parents could end up in jail if the government found the radios we keep under our beds.

Amaro shakes his head and purses his lips. "Mine's better. Before Fidel, your sister could have her quince party with all your family and her bugging you about her new pink dress. After Fidel, your mom can't buy her a dress because it looks too American, so all she does all day is moan and groan in her room. Chicos, seriously. I'm suffering."

Serapio looks at me expectantly. I start to open my mouth but close it. What I want to say is that before Fidel, I could be honest with my friends. After Fidel, I have to lie to them about leaving. Mami and Papi assured me they would get me out of the country before I'm supposed to report to the garrison on July tenth. But they said I shouldn't tell anyone. You never know which of your neighbors has made a hobby of whispering to the Committee for the Defense of the Revolution.

I shake my head, and Serapio groans. "Ay, Cumbito, you never win. All right, chicos. Here's the gold medal, first-place submission. Before Fidel, our teacher was a frog-looking Canadian priest, scared of us superior Cuban boys. But after Fidel, he will return! Replaced by Robo-Padre Tomás! Programmed to inject us with all the ideals of el socialismo."

I swallow hard. If Serapio only knew.

I don't make eye contact with Geraldo, afraid we might reveal something. He already whispered to me yesterday that Padre Tomás had moved on to Havana, but I wasn't supposed to tell anyone. The secrets and whispers wrestle in my brain, giving me a headache.

I start to come to Padre Tomás's defense, but a low rumble fills the air. Serapio, Geraldo, and Amaro look up, trying to find the source of the noise. I look down at my feet, thinking there's an earthquake. Any minute I'll be swallowed into the ground.

The rumble gets louder, and we see an enormous airplane fly overhead. It's a B-52 bomber, just like one of the models in my bedroom that Papi and I built. A flock of white birds flies under the plane.

Squinting, I see they aren't birds. They're pieces of paper. The papers flutter in the air and float to the ground, the only snow I've ever seen in Cuba.

Shouts fill the park as people point to the airplane. Sharp cracks punctuate the shouts. The soldiers, who had been lazily patrolling the park, fire their rifles at the metal monster flying low overhead.

We can hear the bullets from the rifles ricochet off the hull of the airplane, whizzing through the air and pinging off the side. People start to scatter in the park, running away from the firing soldiers.

"Serapito, let's go," I shout as Serapio waves like a maniac to the airplane.

"¡Oye, Yanquis! Drop real Coke next time!" Serapio shouts as I grab him by the arm and pull him away from the square.

Amaro and Geraldo run after us, bumping into each other as they look up at the plane instead of where they are going.

We stampede down a street just far enough from the square that we can still hear the pops of the guns and see the plane circle above Parque Vidal. Amaro sticks out his hand clenched around a crumpled piece of paper. "I got one, guys," he says.

I take the paper from Amaro. "Let me see it."

As I unfold the paper, Amaro, Geraldo, and Serapio huddle around me and read.

¡Ciudadanos cubanos! ¡Lucha por la democracia! ¡América les apoyará!

I mumble the words on the paper. "Cuban citizens! Fight for democracy! America will support you!"

Serapio shrugs. "They should've promised Coke."

"And no school," Amaro says.

"And hamburgers," Geraldo adds. "Isn't that all they eat in the United States?"

I sigh and shove the paper into my pocket. "Like dropping papers is going to get rid of Fidel."

The grumble of the plane fades, and I watch it disappear behind the low roofs and palm trees of Santa Clara, headed toward the United States.

I look back up the street and into Parque Vidal. The soldiers have stopped firing and are now patrolling the perimeter, looking for anyone who snatched up one of the American papers. One solider stands where our street dumps into Parque Vidal and turns toward us, the sneer plastered to his face making him immediately recognizable.

My hand clenches around the paper in my pocket as my knuckles push against the caja de muertos and my breath catches in my throat.

Ignacio narrows his eyes at me and raises his hand, pointing two fingers like a gun. He flicks his wrist like a shot and cackles, his menacing laughter banging against the concrete buildings, tumbling down the street, and slamming into my chest.

CHAPTER 8

I haven't slept in two weeks. Every time I close my eyes, I see Ignacio's black stare. His snarl wraps around my throat and makes it impossible to breathe. The stomp of his heavy boots echoes in my ears and keeps me awake.

Which is probably why I'm about to fall asleep on Dr. Álvarez's examination table. But he jabs another syringe into my hip, and I immediately wake up, clenching the sides of the examination table with my hands.

"Ay caramba," I mutter under my breath.

Dr. Álvarez looks at me over his glasses and purses his lips. "What was that, joven?"

"Nothing, señor," I say.

Dr. Álvarez raises a thick eyebrow and sets the empty syringe on the examination table. "Señor? We don't use that imperialist term anymore. It's *compañero*. Don't you know that?"

"I'm sorry, señor—I mean compañero," I correct myself. "I forgot."

So many rules coming from so many different government committees lately it's easy to forget. The one I always forget says that we should call our fellow Cubans "comrade" instead of "mister" or "miss."

Dr. Álvarez sighs. "Bueno, that's the last of your immunizations. I'm sure you are proud to be joining the Young Rebels."

"Um, sí, compañero," I say, buttoning my pants. "I'm very proud."

When I entered Dr. Álvarez's office this afternoon, I spotted a sign above the doorway. It read, FIDEL, THIS HOUSE IS YOURS. All Cubans faithful to the government hang one in their house or place of business. So I knew I shouldn't tell Dr. Álvarez the real reason for my immunizations.

They are required by the American government to enter the country.

Dr. Álvarez runs his hands through his slicked-back, dark hair. He narrows his eyes at me. "Glad you aren't like one of the gusanos getting shots to leave the country. Had one in here just before you."

He shakes his head. "The cobarde."

I swallow hard and nod, unsure of what to say.

My silence doesn't seem to matter to Dr. Álvarez,

and he continues. "Know what I say? Let them leave."

He waves his hand in the air. "One less mouth to feed. One less gusano to spread their capitalist ideas."

One less innocent person living in fear, I think.

I scan the walls of the examination room. They're lined with pictures of Fidel and Che. A picture next to the door shows two boys a little younger than I am. They're wearing red shorts and white shirts with blue bandannas tied at their necks. Neither is smiling as they salute, hands raised to their foreheads.

Dr. Álvarez clears his throat and walks over to the picture, straightening it with a meaty hand. "Ah, my boys. So proud to be Pioneers."

He scratches his protruding belly. "Your papi must be proud. Just like I am of my boys."

"Sí, compañero. He is." He's proud of my leaving even though he can't quite hide the sadness in his eyes when he thinks I'm not looking.

Dr. Álvarez lowers himself back onto his stool with a grunt. "Can't imagine what the families of those gusanos think. They should all suffer for being such cowards."

I scan his face and watch the drops of sweat roll down his cheeks and rest on his upper lip. "Will the government do anything to the families of the ones that are leaving . . . the gusanos?"

I say a quick prayer that Dr. Álvarez won't realize I'm asking personally.

He pauses from writing on his clipboard and wipes the sweat on his lip with the back of his hand. "Well, if they leave, they leave. The government makes it hard for them to go, but once they're gone"—he pauses and tosses his pen on the examination table—"¡me resbala! Who cares?"

I start to heave a sigh of relief but swallow it.

"Bueno, joven, we're done here," Dr. Álvarez announces, standing and yanking the waistband of his pants over his gut.

"Gracias, Doctor," I say, heading out of the examination room and into the waiting room. My hip is sore from the four shots I received. I try not to limp.

"Ay Dios mío, you'll never walk again!" I hear a voice shout in the waiting room.

Serapio sits on a plastic folding chair and gives me a smirk. "Ay, such a young boy. Cut down in his youth. ¡Qué tragedia!"

The real tragedy is that my friend is completely insane.

"Serapito, what are you doing here?" I ask as Mami walks over to me, rolling her eyes.

Serapio looks back at his abuela and runs his fingers through his hair. "Well, same as you, it seems. Young Rebels, right?"

I shove my hands into my pockets, and Mami puts her arm around my shoulder. "Yep, that's right," I say.

Mami and Papi still don't want me telling my friends I'm leaving. They say it's easier this way. But keeping all this inside makes me feel like a balloon that's been blown up too much. Any second I might just pop.

"Oye, Cumbito, which cheek is better for the shots? Left or right?" Serapio swings his hips side to side as his abuela rises from her chair. She shuffles over and gives him a quick smack on the back of the head.

"I think I'll see if the doctor will sew your mouth shut, no?" Serapio's abuela says, shaking her head.

Mami and I stifle a laugh.

"Buena suerte, Serapito," I say as Mami and I leave, wishing my friend luck. He might need it more with his abuela than he does with the shots.

Mami clenches my hand as we walk home, her heels clicking on the pavement. "Was it really that bad?" she asks.

I sigh. "The shots were nothing compared to Doctor Álvarez's ranting on and on about gusanos."

"Ay, nene, I'm sorry. This will be over soon."

She releases my hand and unsnaps her purse. She points inside. I peek and see a rectangular blue piece of paper stamped with the words PAN AM.

It's my plane ticket.

"Your tío Enrique brought this to me today. He knows people in the American Embassy and was able to get you a student visa, too," Mami says as she snaps her purse shut.

"You have el sastre's passport and education letter. Your immunizations. And now your visa for the United States and your plane ticket." Mami's steps quicken as she marks through her mental checklist. "You have everything you need. You're ready to go."

The pain in my hip increases as I try to keep up with Mami. We pass el sastre's shop and head through Parque Vidal.

I finally think to ask the question that has been burrowing in the back of my mind since I sat on the bed next to Papi.

"When am I leaving?"

Mami takes a deep breath. "July sixth."

Four weeks. I have four more weeks with my family. Four more weeks in my home.

I grab Mami's hand as we walk along the street toward home, the sun setting slowly behind us. Our shadows stretch along the dirt, two figures melting into the horizon. I grip her hand harder, afraid of falling off the edge.

CHAPTER 9

My family is conspiring against me. They've organized The Committee for the Prevention of Cumba Eating.

That is the only explanation for why I'm surrounded by serving trays of steamed white rice, fried sweet plantains, and salty boiled yuca and I haven't had one bite.

My stomach stages a protest and growls again, but I'm forced to ignore it. Mami sent me on a mission to help Abuelo organize the chairs in our backyard. We've cleared our house of every chair and moved them outside to have enough seating for all the family that's descended on our house. We're having a party for Mami's birthday. At least, that's what the gossipy neighbors will think. Really, it's a going-away party for me. But Mami's birthday is in a week, so that's our cover.

As I return from helping Abuelo, Mami hands me

another glass of water. I know it's her cure-all, but I think she's trying to turn me into a fish so I can just swim to the United States.

"Gracias, Mami," I say, gulping down the water.

My arms still ache from the work I did this morning with Abuelo, Papi, and his brother, Tío Carlos. Burying a pig in the ground is a four-man job. By the time we got the hole deep enough, sweat had completely soaked through our shirts.

This morning, Tío Carlos brought over the already butchered pig from his farm. The best way to make lechón is to dig a hole in the ground and bury the pig with hot coals covered in banana leaves. When the pig is pulled out, the skin is crispy and salty and the meat inside is juicy.

It's my favorite food. And my family seems determined to keep me from enjoying it.

"Mami, I need water, too," Pepito whines. He supervised our work this morning but somehow managed to avoid touching a shovel, instead building a miniature bulldozer with my Erector set.

"Ay, nene, you're fine," Tía Carmen says, swatting Pepito with a towel. She grabs a large serving bowl and holds it while Mami fills it with steaming black beans. The smell of garlic, peppers, and vinegar makes my mouth water.

Mami moves to a large pot on the stove and ladles out a small bowl of ajiaco.

Pepito moans. "Ajiaco again? Mami, you only make soup."

Mami raises an eyebrow at Pepito and points the soup ladle to the trays of guava pastries, sweet rice pudding, and fried ham croquetas. She hands me the bowl of soup. "Take this to your tía Margarita. She must be hungry."

Tía Margarita is pregnant, her swollen belly barely fitting through the doorway when she arrived with Tío Carlos this morning. I got a smack on the back of the head from Abuela when I mentioned it.

I walk out into the backyard with the hot bowl of ajiaco, carefully eyeing the swaying broth with each step I take. I spot Tía Margarita in a corner sitting on one of the kitchen chairs we moved out into the yard, her feet propped up on another chair. She's fanning herself with her hands, the movement doing little to keep the mosquitoes away.

Right before I get to her, I trip on a root from the bougainvillea bush growing in our backyard. The ajiaco slops in the bowl and spills out onto my hand. I wince as the hot broth stings my fingers.

"¡Ay, pobrecito!" Tía Margarita exclaims, taking the bowl and setting it on the ground. She grabs my throbbing red hand and begins to rub it, muttering, "Sana sana, colita de rana, si no te sanas hoy, te sanarás mañana."

I smirk as she continues mumbling her superstitious cure about a frog's tail. "I'm okay, Tía," I say as my stomach grumbles. "Really, it's fine."

Tía Margarita keeps rubbing my hand. "Remember, Cumba, if you cross your sandals by your bed," she says, crossing her fingers into an x, "then you won't have bad dreams when you go to the United States. Do you still have your azabache? You should take that for good luck."

I'm not sure Tía's suggestion will work. The azabache is a charm that most Cuban babies wear to ward off the evil eye, but I've got a domino in my pocket that proves bad luck will find you no matter what.

"Thank you, Tía," I say anyway. "I need to go back and help Mami."

I make my way across the backyard, following the pungent smell of lechón drifting from the kitchen. I keep my eyes trained on the heaping tray of starchy yuca.

"Cumba, wait a second," Tío Enrique says, grabbing my arm.

The Committee for the Prevention of Cumba Eating strikes again.

"Yes, Tío?" I sigh. My stomach growls in protest.

Tío Enrique motions for me to sit down with him and Tía Rosita at one of the tables we moved to the backyard.

I sit and stare as Tía Rosita digs into her enormous plate of black beans, steamed white rice, and lechón. My mouth starts to water.

"Cumba, we want to give you something before you leave for the United States," Tío Enrique says, snapping me from my roast-pork trance.

He reaches into his pocket and withdraws a shiny gold watch. He hands it to me, and I inspect the face. A gold crown and the word ROLEX stare back up at me.

"Tío, this is a really nice watch. I can't take it," I say, holding the watch out to him.

Tío Enrique closes my hand around the watch. "You'll need money in the United States. This is a good thing to sell."

Tía Rosita nods as she shovels another forkful of black beans and rice into her mouth.

"Mami!" two girls cry in unison as they run up to us. Cuquita and Maricela, Tío and Tía's twin daughters, tug on their mother's green dress. I spot sticky red guava paste at the corners of their mouths.

"Can we have more croquetas and pastelitos?" they whine, shaking their curly black hair.

More? I haven't even had *one*!

"Sí, niñas. And bring me a bowl of rice pudding, too," Tía Rosita replies.

Arroz con leche, too? When I get to the United States, I'm going to have a whole huge meal and eat whatever I want, as much as I want.

All by myself.

Tía Rosita smiles at me and unclasps the string of small white pearls from her neck.

"We want you to have this, too, Cumba," she says, handing me the necklace. "You should be able to get quite a bit for it as well."

I feel a twinge of guilt for being annoyed at Tío and Tía. They may be keeping me from pastelitos and lechón, but their generosity puts a lump in my throat.

"Gracias," I tell them, placing the watch and necklace in my pocket and rising from my chair.

"We'll be praying for you, niño," Tía Rosita says, patting my hand. "How are you feeling about leaving?"

I stare at the wandering vines and flowers on the tablecloth. How do I tell them that I feel like I'm being held over an endless abyss, the last string about to be cut?

I shrug. "Okay, I guess. If you'll excuse me, I need

to go help Mami." And fill a plate with all the beans, rice, yuca, and lechón my stomach can hold.

As I'm about to go back into the house, Papi, Abuelo, and Tío Carlos burst out of the doorway, instruments in hand.

Papi slaps me on the back and waves his clarinet in the air. "Come, Cumba. Come listen."

The Committee strikes a third time. Aaaaand I'm out.

I sit next to Pepito and watch as Abuelo strums his guitar and Tío Carlos taps on his bongos. Papi raises his clarinet to his lips, launching into a traditional Cuban melody. Behind me, Abuela claps her hands and sings, "Guantanamera, guajira, guantanamera."

I look at the faces in the backyard smiling and singing. Pepito pats his hand to the rhythm on my knee. Mami swings her hips side to side, her blue skirt swaying to the music. The twins are holding hands, spinning in a circle as Tía Rosita sings along with Tía Margarita.

This is my family. And I'm leaving them in five days.

I don't feel so hungry anymore.

I pat Pepito on the back and get up from my chair, heading into the house.

I spot Manuelito sitting by himself in Mami's dentist chair at the front of our house. He's throwing a shiny gold cylinder up in the air and catching it.

"What are you doing in here?" I ask.

"Cuquita and Maricela keep asking me to play tea party with them. Not happening," Manuelito responds, throwing the metal object in the air. He catches it and gives me a smirk.

"So you all packed and ready to run away like a cobarde?"

I raise my hands in the air. "Just give it a rest, Manuelito. You're gonna have to find someone new to torture while I'm gone. If I find out it's Pepito . . ." I pause, realizing there won't be anything I can do, miles away in the United States.

"Whatever," Manuelito sighs. He clenches the metal piece in his fist.

I pull up Mami's examination chair and sit next to him. "What is that?"

Manuelito opens his hand. "A bullet casing. From a rifle, I think. Found it in Parque Vidal."

We sit in silence staring at the empty bullet. Out in the backyard, Papi's clarinet runs a scale and Tío Carlos increases his rhythm on the bongos. Mami's laughter floats above the music.

Manuelito clears his throat. "So, when you go to

the United States"—he pauses, fiddling with the casing between his fingers—"do you think there will be a lot of other Cubans?"

I shrug. "I don't know. Prima Benita is picking me up at the airport. I'm definitely not the first Cuban to leave, but Papi said there aren't a lot of us in Miami. It's mostly blanquitos who don't speak Spanish."

Manuelito stares at me, his brown eyes searching my face. I realize what he wants me to say.

"Miami's a big city. Bigger than Havana. The chances of running into your dad—"

"I know," Manuelito says, cutting me off. He shoves the bullet casing into his pocket. "I guess when some people leave, they just stay gone."

His eyes begin to water. I put my hand on his shoulder.

"Somebody once told me you never really leave. But maybe you do. Maybe you have to forget where you come from so you can bear being in a new place."

Even as I say the words, I know they're not true.

CHAPTER 10

I wish I could take pictures with my mind so that I would never forget. I want to remember how the royal palms stretch to the sky. Demonio's sneaky footprints in the dirt outside our house. The small tear in Abuelo's hat, always perched on his head. Papi's clarinet resting on his leg.

I want to remember Cuba.

Rearranging the folded clothes in my suitcase for the tenth time, my shaking hands wrinkle their fabric.

It's July sixth. I'm leaving.

I sit on my bed next to my suitcase and stare at the room Pepito and I share. He's taped magazine pictures of cowboys and American movie stars to the wall next to his bed. I want to take one of the pictures and tuck it between the two pairs of pants in my suitcase. I want to pack my model of a P-51 Mustang that Papi and I built together and the architecture book my abuelos gave me for my last birthday. I think about creeping into Mami's room and taking her bottle of lavender perfume. I look at the size of my suitcase. How many of Abuela's croquetas and pastelitos could I fit inside?

How do you pack twelve years of memories?

I hear a shuffle coming down the hallway, and Mami appears at the door. Her hair is carefully done and her dress freshly ironed. She's taken care to look her best to take me to the airport. Papi is getting Tío Enrique's car right now.

She clears her throat and holds out a small photo to me. "I thought you might want to take this with you. If you put it in your pocket, maybe they won't notice," she says softly.

I take the photo and run my fingers along the edge. It's a picture of Papi, Mami, Pepito, and me. I smile as I look at Pepito's silly grin as he stands proudly dressed in the cowboy costume Tío Enrique and Tía Rosita bought him. I slip it into my pocket, and my fingers jam against the caja de muertos.

Mami opens her mouth to say something, but a sharp knock at our front door echoes through the house.

I start to follow Mami down the hall, but she waves her hand. "You should stay in your room."

I lean on the doorframe, out of sight of the front door of our house. I hear Mami open the door and let out a sharp gasp.

Looking down the hallway, I see Pepito sitting at our kitchen table. His eyes grow wide, and the blood drains from his face. I watch as his fingers clench the edge of the table and his knee starts to bounce up and down. Abuela gets up from her chair and stands behind Pepito, pressing her hands on his shoulders to keep him from fidgeting.

The voice at the front door rises. "It doesn't matter what day I said. Your son comes to the garrison now!"

Ignacio.

I lock eyes with Abuelo as he sits at the kitchen table. He lowers his newspaper and smooths the pages with his hand. Looking toward the front door, he says, "I'm afraid that won't be possible today, compañero. Poor Cumba is very sick."

I hear Ignacio grunt. He clearly doesn't believe Abuelo.

I press my hands against the hallway walls, my knees shaking. This can't be happening.

Abuelo stands and faces Ignacio, straightening his shoulders. "Perhaps if you come in four days, the day you originally requested, he will be better by then."

"I don't think you want to take a sick child to a garrison full of brave soldiers," Mami says, her voice unsteady. "He could infect them all. How would that further the ideals of our glorious revolution?"

Ignacio pushes past Mami and into our house. He barges through the kitchen and shoves a chair out of his way, knocking it to the tile floor with a hard thud.

I'm paralyzed in the hallway. My hands shake at my sides, and my throat burns. I was so close. Today was the day I was meant to escape.

Ignacio stomps down the hallway and towers above me, his chest heaving and his hand gripping the black pistol at his side. "You're coming with me," he growls.

My stomach clenches, and tears prick the corners of my eyes. Hot liquid scorches my throat as my face burns. I can feel it coming, and I can't stop it.

I throw up on Ignacio's boots.

Mami races toward me and gathers me in her arms, my legs finally giving out. She brushes my hair off my sweat-soaked forehead. "See, I told you he was sick," she says to Ignacio. "There is no way he can go to the garrison today."

Ignacio narrows his eyes at me, looking me up and down. My stomach starts to gurgle again, and I cough, hot bile dripping from my lips and spraying the front of Ignacio's uniform.

Taking a step back, Ignacio releases his hand from his pistol.

Abuelo clears his throat behind him. "Compañero, let's leave the ladies to care for him, no? I can walk with you back to the garrison. Perhaps we can stop and have those boots shined."

Ignacio looks at Mami and points his finger at me. "The tenth. He'd better be there."

Mami nods. "I promise he will," she says, squeezing my arms. Her hands shake, but her voice is steady.

Abuelo puts his hand on Ignacio's shoulder, leading him away from us, through the kitchen, past Mami's dental office, and out the front door. I shrug off Mami's grip and stumble to the front of the house.

"Nene, wait!" Abuela exclaims as I grip the doorframe, my legs still shaking.

I watch as Abuelo walks with Ignacio down the dusty street away from me. I want to scream for him to turn around. I want to wrap my arms around him one more time before I go.

Of all the things Fidel has taken from me, this has been the worst.

He won't even let me say goodbye.

CHAPTER 11

As we drive from Santa Clara to the airport in Havana, I watch the sun climb above the hills. When Mami told Papi what happened that morning with Ignacio, the nervous look they exchanged made my stomach roll all over again. Pepito's nervous chatter does little to calm my nerves as Papi guides the borrowed car down the hills toward Havana.

We pull up to José Martí International Airport, named after the herald of Cuban freedom who will usher me into a new world. To new freedom.

Pepito doesn't care about that. He doesn't let go of my hand as we get out of the car and head into the airport.

We stop before a line of armed guards searching passengers getting on the planes. Mami fixes the collar of my shirt for the hundredth time, and I pretend not to notice that her hands shake more each time she does it.

"You need to look your best," she says, patting down my collar. "And represent Cuba well."

"I know, Mami," I say, searching her face and memorizing the way her eyelashes curl upward and how she reaches for the cross at her neck with her red fingernails every time she's nervous.

"Of course you know. You're a smart boy."

She starts to say something else but stops and pulls me into a tight hug, undoing all the care she took ironing my suit this morning.

I breathe in her lavender perfume and close my eyes, rubbing my hand against the smooth fabric of her dress. She squeezes me tighter.

Papi clears his throat, and Mami releases me. He warned us about making a scene at the airport. As far as the guards are concerned, I'm a student going to study in the United States for a few months. At least that's what the letter el sastre forged says.

Pepito still holds on to my hand, his nails digging into my palm as he stares at the pistols secured to the guards' hips.

Mami starts to fiddle with the gold cross around her neck again as Papi steps toward me. He places his hand on my shoulder.

"You have your passport?" he asks.

"Yes, Papi." I say a small prayer that el sastre's

bragging was justified and that the guards won't be able to spot the forgery.

He grips my shoulder. "You packed a tooth-brush?"

"Of course, Papi."

He's stalling. I know it. But I could stand here forever feeling the warm heat from his hand, memorizing the few strands of gray hair at his temples.

"Prima Benita will meet you at the airport in Miami. She'll be waiting for you."

"I know."

I catch Mami wiping the corner of her eye with a finger and take a deep breath. There's so much I want to say to them. But we're in a fishbowl, guards staring at us, their hands resting on their pistols as they scowl at passengers.

Papi stares at me. I know he's trying to think of another question to ask. Something else to prolong this moment. We stand in silence, the bustle of the airport around us muted by my heart beating in my ears.

Pepito squeezes my hand. "Oye, Cumbito. You'll buy me a cowboy hat when you get to the United States?"

I chuckle. "Of course, Pepito. I hear everyone wears them."

I give him a wink. Papi releases his grip on my shoulder and pulls Pepito to his side.

"I guess you'd better go," Papi says.

Pepito drops my hand and wraps his arms around Mami's waist.

I take a deep breath. "Will you tell Abuelo and Abuela . . ." I try to finish, but my voice catches in my throat and my chin starts to quiver.

"See you soon," Mami says, the tears in her eyes threatening to spill over as they dart to the soldiers standing around us.

"Yes, see you soon," Papi says firmly.

Pepito buries his head in Mami's side.

"I'll get you that cowboy hat, Pepito. Promise." I can't think of anything else to say.

Anything but goodbye.

I give my parents a weak smile and turn toward the guards.

I hear my mother call after me, "See you soon."

I swallow hard and say a small prayer of hope that she's right.

Passing through a line of guards dressed in their typical green fatigues and stern faces, I hand my ticket, Ministry of Education letter, and passport to a guard perched behind a podium. He inspects the documents. My tongue feels swollen in my mouth as I watch his eyes scan over my birth date and the forged official seal.

He slaps a stamp down on the first blank page of my passport and passes it back to me, waving me on with a grunt.

God bless you, el sastre.

I move to another guard waiting with an even deeper scowl on his face. He motions for me to place my suitcase on a table in front of him.

"Going to study in the United States?" he asks as I heft my small suitcase onto the table. His dark eyes scan me up and down.

"Yes," I say, hoping my voice doesn't sound nervous. I scan the waiting area, expecting to see Ignacio burst in and call me a liar as he drags me back to Santa Clara.

The guard opens my suitcase and begins to root around inside. I shove my hand into my pocket and rub the caja de muertos. I try not to stare at the pair of underwear I wrapped around the watch and pearls that Tío Enrique and Tía Rosita gave me.

The guard starts to take my clothes out of my suitcase and throws them onto the table. He tosses the pair of underwear I'd tightly rolled around my contraband, and they land with a hard clank.

The guard raises a thick eyebrow at me, unfolding

the underwear. Tío Enrique's watch and Tía Rosita's pearls lay exposed between us.

The guard smirks. "Studying in the United States? Qué tontería. You're a niño bitongo."

He spits out the last two words. *Niño bitongo* is what Fidel calls all the children who are leaving, who are being sent alone by their parents to a new country. He calls us spoiled brats for wanting to be free of the revolution.

The guard picks up the watch and necklace. I feel sweat starting to drop down my forehead, but I'm too afraid to wipe it away. I keep my hands shoved in my pockets, my fist clenched around the domino as the corners cut into my palm.

"If you're studying in the United States, you won't be needing these," the guard says as he deposits the watch and necklace into the chest pocket of his fatigues.

He eyes my hand in my pocket. "What have you got there?"

I swallow hard and take my hand out of my pocket. Opening my palm to reveal the domino, I look away from the guard, embarrassed at how much my hand is shaking.

The guard raises an eyebrow. "A caja de muertos, eh? That bad luck you can keep."

He smiles and reveals a row of crooked yellow teeth.

Stuffing my clothes back in, the guard shoves my suitcase at me. He rests his hand on the black pistol at his side, and my throat closes. I try to suck in a breath and choke on my tongue.

"Run, worm," the guard snarls, his grip tightening around the handle of the pistol as his dark eyes burn into my skin.

Black spots float in my eyes as I try to breathe. "What?" I gasp.

"Run. Run before I shoot you like the coward you are."

The corners of the guard's lips curl up, as if waiting to taste my blood.

I grab my suitcase and push out the door, the heat slamming into my entire body. My legs shake, and I stumble on the tarmac. The airplane looms before me, a tall staircase leading up to the door, where a stewardess is waiting. I breathe a sigh of relief and turn to see if I can spot Papi, Mami, and Pepito still in the airport. I want to give them just one wave goodbye to let them know I'll be okay.

But I can't see them through all the guards milling around.

I'm so busy looking back into the airport that I

bump into the person in front of me and fall to the ground.

I untangle my legs and arms from a sniffling girl wearing a green plaid dress. She looks a little younger than Pepito, and her eyes are rimmed with red.

"Ay, perdón," I apologize, helping her up. She looks at me and grabs her blue suitcase, struggling to carry it.

"Do you need help?" I ask.

"I need my mami," she responds, wiping a snotty nose with the back of her hand.

I grab her suitcase with my other hand. "C'mon. We can go together."

She tromps up the stairs in front of me, her long braids swinging side to side, as I lug our suitcases. The stewardess at the top of the stairs greets us with a perky smile.

She says something in English, nodding at each of us and pointing into the airplane.

The little girl turns and looks at me. I shrug. I should've paid better attention during Padre Tomás's English lessons.

We stand at the top of the stairs waiting for instructions from a woman we can't understand. A dark-suited man behind us clears his throat. "Vamos, niños. Apúrense."

We follow the man's instructions and hurry into the plane. Watching the other passengers place their suitcases in compartments over the seats, I do the same with the girl's bag. I shove my luggage next to hers and take my seat beside her.

"You'll be okay," I reassure her as she continues to sniffle, wiping her hands on the skirt of her dress.

"I was okay with my mami and papi," she mumbles, lowering her head and crossing her arms.

The stewardess at the front of the plane announces something in English, and I see the passengers around me buckle their seat belts.

I look at the two metal clasps on my lap and wonder how they're supposed to secure together and keep me from bouncing like a pinball around the airplane cabin.

I watch the man across the aisle and finally figure out how to join the two pieces. Looking at the little girl next to me, I see that she has knotted together the straps that hold the buckles.

"No, that's not how you do it," I say, untying the straps. I buckle her seat belt, and she wiggles down farther in her seat, chin still buried in her chest.

The plane's engines start to roar, and the little girl jumps in her seat. The plane starts to move forward, and as it increases speed, she grabs my hand. I feel my back press into my seat as the plane begins to lift. My stomach stays on the ground.

"Are you sure it's going to be okay?" she asks, squeezing my hand tighter.

I want to tell her yes. But how do I know if everything is going to be okay? I don't have some magic crystal ball that can tell the future.

As the plane lifts higher in the air, I look out the window past the little girl and watch the rocky shore of my homeland give way to vast blue water.

I say a prayer that Fidel's hand won't reach out of the sea and yank the plane back to Cuba.

Just let us leave, Fidel. You don't need us, I think over and over as land disappears behind us and we fly ahead into the unknown.

CHAPTER 12

Dots of islands scatter across the sea as our plane continues its journey. The islands grow thicker and larger and eventually give way to solid land.

The little girl, whose name I've learned is Adelita, squirms next to me and presses her nose to the window.

"Is that . . . ?"

"Yes," I reply. "It's the United States."

We begin to descend, and Adelita points out the window. Tall buildings line the coast, scattered with specs of people.

I wonder if they are kind.

I wonder if they speak Spanish.

I wonder if they care that two children have flown by themselves from the only home they've ever known.

The palm trees and buildings race closer to the bottom of our plane as we continue our descent. Adelita grabs my hand again as my ears pop.

The wheels of the plane touch ground with a screech, and a rushing sound fills the cabin as the pilot slows us down.

I'm here. I made it. I want to tell Mami. I want to tell Papi that I'm safe.

But they're across the sea, far away.

Adelita and I grab our suitcases and follow the other passengers into the airport. It's a large metal hangar much nicer than the crumbling concrete airport in Havana.

There are signs all over the airport, but neither of us know what they say. We follow the sea of passengers getting off the plane and end up in front of a woman behind a podium. Her mouth is in a permanent line, and she narrows her eyes when she sees us. This doesn't bother me, because, unlike the men behind podiums at the Havana airport, she doesn't have a gun.

She sticks out an open palm to me and says, "*Whatsyourname?*"

I scrunch my eyebrows together. I should know what she's saying. It sounds familiar.

The woman sighs loudly and rolls her eyes. "*Whatsyourname?*"

Adelita nudges my elbow. "She wants to know your name," she explains in Spanish.

"Oh, Cumba Fernandez," I tell the woman.

She stamps my passport and hands it back to me. Adelita answers the woman's question quickly when it's her turn, and we head into the reception area.

"I got all high marks in English at school," she says, puffing out her chest.

"Good for you. I didn't do that well. I sat next to someone who tried to convince our teacher that we only spoke German."

We push through the crowd of people in the airport. I look around and notice there aren't any soldiers with guns.

"¡Ay, mira! So many legs," Adelita exclaims.

She's right. Half the people milling around the reception area are wearing shorts. Even the women. They must not have gotten cocotazos from their mamis before they left their houses this morning. Even in the hottest weather, my family, and probably Adelita's, wore dress pants and dresses. That's just how Cubans dress. Evidently, the same doesn't apply to Americans.

I search the faces in the reception area and realize I don't know what Prima Benita looks like. Papi told me she was my cousin, but that doesn't exactly help. We use that term for people who are so distantly related, their family tree is in another forest.

Maybe I should just find the kindest-looking old lady and go with her. I should definitely find one who looks like she speaks Spanish, as if our language is scrawled across our foreheads and not in the confused looks we give people around us.

"Cumba?"

I feel a hand on my shoulder and turn to come face-to-face with a short, gray-haired woman the same age as Abuela.

"Cumba Fernandez?" she asks again.

"Sí, that's me. Prima Benita?"

The woman claps her hands together. "Ay, niño. I'm so glad you're here," she says in Spanish.

She smiles, and the wrinkles on her face deepen.

I let out a deep breath. Prima Benita brushes her stubby fingers along my cheek, and I blink back tears.

"It's okay, niño. You're safe now," she says, her golden eyes sparkling.

I want to hug her and bury myself in her brown dress.

Adelita scuffs her feet beside me and clears her throat. "Are you here for me, too?"

Prima Benita looks Adelita up and down and places a hand on her head. "I'm sorry, mi niña, I don't think I am. Do you know who's supposed to pick you up?"

Adelita's chest starts to heave, and her knuckles turn white from the death grip she has on her suitcase.

"No, I don't know. I don't know. They just put me on the plane. I don't know."

Prima Benita pulls Adelita to her side and rubs her back. "Don't worry. We'll figure it out."

I give Prima Benita a weak smile and shrug. She looks around the airport as Adelita sniffles into her shoulder.

A nun dressed in light blue approaches us and says something in English. Prima Benita responds and pulls Adelita from her side.

"This woman is here to pick you up, mi niña," she says, brushing Adelita's hair back. "See? There's no need to worry."

I look at the nun, whose hair is pulled back so tightly under her habit her eyebrows are frozen in astonishment. She hasn't smiled once. I'm not certain she has teeth.

"Come," the nun says to Adelita, snapping her fingers.

"It's okay," I reassure Adelita. "My abuelo says we won't be here long. You'll be all right."

The nun purses her lips at me, not understanding my Spanish, and snaps at Adelita again.

Adelita shuffles away, clutching her suitcase to her chest.

Prima Benita and I watch them walk away as the nun snaps her long, bony fingers at two boys, who get up and follow her with their suitcases. Adelita looks back at me and wipes away the tears from her cheek. I give her a half-hearted thumbs-up.

"Do you think that's true?" Prima Benita asks. "What your abuelo said?"

I look down at the ground and scuff my feet. "I don't know. But it sounded good at the time, didn't it?"

"I suppose," she says, patting me on the back. "Come, let's go. I want to hear all about how your mami and papi are doing. Is my foolish cousin still climbing coconut trees?"

I chuckle as we walk out of the airport, even though my chest tightens at Prima Benita's mention of Abuelo. The Miami sun bears down on us as we walk to her car, and I squint.

Prima Benita stops in front of a cherry-red Chevrolet Bel Air, just like I've seen in the movies. The roof is a spotless white, and the trunk has fins that make it look like the car might fly away at any moment.

Sliding into the driver's seat, she strains her feet to reach the pedals as she cranes her neck above the steering wheel. Prima Benita slams on the accelerator and backs up the huge boat of a car, exclaiming, "¡Ay!"

We speed out of the airport, Prima Benita peering down her nose over the steering wheel. She weaves in and out of traffic, and I'm afraid she's driving purely on faith. It would be a shame to escape Fidel's clutches only to die in a horrific car accident at the hands of a short, elderly Cuban woman.

As Prima Benita winds through the streets of Miami, the buildings and palm trees blur past the car window. I begin to blink as her soft voice fills the car. I don't hear what she's saying. My head leans against the window as we pass block after block of this new city. My suit weighs a hundred pounds, and my body finally gives up.

A gentle nudge on my arm wakes me.

"We're here, niño," Prima Benita says, pointing to a small light-blue house in front of us. White decorative bars cover the windows, and red flowers line the front porch.

I stretch as I get out of the car and look down the street. It's filled with small, pastel-colored houses. It doesn't look that much different from my street in Cuba. The houses are made of the same thick concrete, built to withstand any storm. There's a poinciana tree outside Prima Benita's house with bright orange blossoms, just like my house in Santa Clara. I spot a brown cat that could be Demonio's twin jump down from the front porch and meander up the walk to greet us.

There are so many things that are the same. There's just one important difference.

This isn't home.

CHAPTER 13

I don't know where I am.

Opening my eyes, I kick the blanket off my body. There's a soft snore coming from the bed across the room, but it's not Pepito. The whir of the air conditioner perched in the window tells me I'm not in my own bedroom.

I sit up and remember. Mami's tears, Papi's questions. The plane soaring over the sea.

I'm in the United States.

I gather some clothes from the short wooden dresser between the beds and shuffle to the bathroom in Prima Benita's house. Splashing cold water on my face, I try to wake up. Yesterday still hangs on my shoulders.

I change out of my pajamas and into a pair of pants and a short-sleeved shirt. I don't want to change in the bedroom. It feels weird with a stranger in there.

Alejandro, my roommate, just grunted at me when Prima Benita showed me our bedroom yesterday. He sat on his bed playing with a small radio and didn't look up when we were introduced. Prima Benita said he was seventeen and from Matanzas. I wonder if he had to join the Young Rebels or even the military before he was able to leave.

I walk into the kitchen and find Prima Benita at the stove, her gray hair piled on top of her head. She stirs a pot of light-colored mud, the silver cross around her neck dangling above the sludge. At least, that's what it looks like. It has no smell.

"Buenos días, señora," I say, taking a seat at the small kitchen table. Light from a large window seeps through white shutters. I rub my eyes. I think I could've easily slept another day.

"Good morning, Cumba," she says, setting a bowl of the mystery sludge in front of me. "Make sure you say 'good morning' in English from now on. You need to practice before school starts."

My stomach drops. School in the United States. I hadn't thought of that. At least I have two months of freedom before facing that new challenge.

I pick up my spoon and poke at the beige glob in the bowl.

"It's oatmeal," Prima Benita says, sensing my reluctance.

"Oat . . . meal?" I mimic her English.

She pushes a small bowl of brown sugar toward me and smiles. "It's better with this."

I take a spoon and sprinkle some brown sugar on the oatmeal as Alejandro emerges from the bathroom, dressed in pants and a button-down shirt. He slouches in his seat and blows his long black bangs out of his eyes with a sigh. I notice a scar that runs from the corner of his eyebrow to his temple. He catches me staring and brushes his hair in front of it.

"Sit up, please," Prima Benita says, setting a bowl of oatmeal in front of him and opening her large Bible. Its brown leather cover is well-worn and torn at the edges, probably from years of use from Prima Benita's work as a missionary for the Methodist Church.

Alejandro sits up and adds four heaping spoonfuls of brown sugar to his oatmeal. I taste my oatmeal and decide I should have done the same. It tastes like warm glue.

Prima Benita begins reading to us from her Bible as we eat, first from the left column, which is written in English, and then from the right, in Spanish. I recognize only a handful of the English words she says. It's a relief when she reads the Spanish.

I manage to stomach my entire bowl of oatmeal.

I could've stopped after the first bite, but I don't want to be rude. It sits like wet cement in my stomach.

I think of the food Mami and Abuela would always have on the table for breakfast: thick slices of mango dripping with juice and fresh chunks of bread slathered with sticky guava paste. I grip the edge of the table and blink, trying not to let tears fall for things that are far away, out of my reach.

Alejandro scrapes his bowl clean and tosses the spoon onto the table. Prima Benita raises her eyebrow at him, and he places the spoon in the bowl.

"So, what do you boys have planned today?" she asks, closing her Bible and rubbing her hand on the cover.

I sit in silence and glance at Alejandro. I don't have any plans. And from the scowl on his face, it looks like he doesn't want to have any plans with me. I shrug.

Prima Benita grabs a large green cracker tin from above the stove and opens it at the table. "Well, here's some spending money you can take with you today. You should explore your new city," she says, giving me a wink.

She slides two silver coins across the table to me and does the same for Alejandro. He grabs the money and shoves it into his pocket, grunting what I assume is supposed to be a thank-you.

I pick up the coins in front of me. My own money. Comandante Che tried to outlaw money in Cuba as part of the socialist government. And now I'm rubbing two American coins between my fingers.

"Thank you," I say, taking time to enunciate my English as well as I can.

Alejandro and I wash our bowls and place them by the kitchen sink to dry before heading out the door. He walks down the sidewalk in front of me, his shoulders slumped and his hands in his pockets. I follow a few steps behind him, feeling the coins bounce in one pocket of my pants as the caja de muertos bounces in the other. One pocket has the United States, the other Cuba.

Alejandro turns quickly on his heels, and I almost slam into him. "You're not following me," he says.

"I . . . I wasn't following you," I stammer. "I just don't know where to go."

"Anywhere," Alejandro says, waving his arms. "Miami is a big city. Lots to explore. You don't need to follow me around like a lost dog."

He turns and stomps away from me, his hands once again shoved in his pockets. I stand in the middle of the sidewalk and look up and down Prima

Benita's street. Miami is so much bigger than Santa Clara, a maze of streets, bridges, and highways waiting to tangle me in their concrete tentacles. But I guess the opposite direction from Alejandro will have to do for today.

I walk up the street, admiring the small houses, their flower gardens, and the American cars parked out front. A blue Chrysler Windsor with enormous back fins. A green Ford Fairlane with whitewall tires. A brown Dodge Lancer with a sparkling silver grille.

I feel like I'm in one of the American movies that Serapio, Amaro, Geraldo, and I used to go see at the theater near Parque Vidal.

I wander until my feet ache, up and down streets and past buildings whose English signs I can't read. If I had walked this long in Santa Clara, I would've reached the ocean. But here it's street after street of buildings and the occasional palm tree. In all my walking, I don't see a single soldier. Not a single gun. No one is marching down the street, shouting with their fists raised.

I turn a corner and arrive at a white building with a glass front. Above the building, large orange letters announce ROYAL CASTLE. I don't know what that means, but the smell coming from the building makes my mouth water. I'm dying to get the taste of "oatmeal" out of my mouth.

Grabbing the two coins from my pocket, I push through the door.

A tall man nods at me from behind a long orange counter and motions for me to sit on one of the white plastic stools lining it. I look up at the menu hanging above the counter and scan the signs for any words I recognize. Luckily, the menu has pictures as well.

Settling in my seat, I mentally go over how I'm going to order. I'm so busy practicing in my head, I don't notice the man standing in front of me, tapping his pencil on his order pad.

He says something in English and smiles, his blue eyes and freckles making him stand out like an alien. I have no idea what he just said. I search his face for clues and read the name tag pinned to his orange apron, declaring that he's Marvin.

"*WhatcanIgetyou?*" he repeats.

Why do people have to talk so quickly? Are they all in a hurry?

I give him my practiced speech. "Hamburger. Coke. Please."

Setting my two coins on the counter, I realize I have no idea how much money I have.

Marvin scribbles on his pad and passes it through the counter behind him to the kitchen.

I try to hand him my two coins, but he wipes his hands on his orange apron and raises his eyebrows.

He says something in English again. I stare at his pale lips, trying to understand.

Marvin smiles and slides one of the coins toward me. He takes the other coin and holds it up. "Twenty-five," he says.

My eyes grow big. I know that number!

I put the coin in my pocket. The man takes the other coin, walks over to the cash register, and hits a button, opening the cash drawer. He deposits my coin and takes out a smaller silver coin.

Setting this coin in front of me, he says, "Ten."

I know that number, too. Never mind that Serapio made me learn it in German as well.

I give the man a big smile. "Thank you," I say, knowing that my pronunciation makes it sound more like "tank you."

Marvin sets down my hamburger and Coke in front of me. I unwrap the hamburger from its white paper. Steam rises to my face, and I breathe in. The first bite sends hot juice down my chin, and I wipe it away with the back of my hand.

I take a gulp of the Coke. The bubbles tickle my throat. Real Coke, unlike the garbage Not Coke that Che tried to make.

Marvin laughs and slaps me on the shoulder. He says something in English I can't understand, but the huge smile on his face makes me feel at ease.

He takes his order pad from his apron and rips off a paper. He scribbles something on the back, setting the paper in front of me.

"Hamburger. Ten cents," he says, pointing to the words on the paper with his pencil. "Coke. Five cents."

I take my two American coins out of my pocket and set them on the table. I point to the small silver one and say, "Ten?"

Marvin smiles, his blue eyes glinting. A large man in the kitchen shouts something to him, but Marvin waves him off.

I point to the larger silver coin and say cautiously, "Twenty-five?"

Marvin laughs and gives me a thumbs-up.

My first English lesson in the United States. And it comes with a juicy hamburger and real Coke.

I thumb the coins in my palm and think of Adelita. I wonder if the sour nun has let her try hamburgers. I wonder if she has her own bedroom or if she has to share.

I wonder if she's just realized how homesick she is.

CHAPTER 14

Dear Pepito,

People in Miami don't wear cowboy hats. They don't wear cowboy boots. They look a lot like people in Cuba. I passed a woman yesterday who looked so much like Doña Teresa I had to look twice to make sure Demonio wasn't following her. But if you look at people in the United States long enough, you see they aren't anything like people in Cuba. They walk a little taller, their shoulders held back, not hunched over. Their eyes don't dart up and down the street, looking for soldiers with guns. They don't have worry etched into every line on their faces. And they don't speak Spanish.

That last part is the biggest difference.

I'm trying to learn, but everyone speaks so quickly. I think they're afraid they'll forget what they're going to say if they don't shove the words out of their mouths as soon as possible. It's like an English train, barreling down the track at full speed. I'm lucky if I can catch a car. But I'll most likely just be run over.

Every day I walk to a restaurant called Royal Castle. Marvin, the man who works there, is teaching me English. I don't always get it right, but he's very patient. And an American hamburger and Coke can soothe a mountain of mistakes. He brings books his daughter reads. They're baby books. I guess I speak baby English. We look at the pictures together, and Marvin tells me the English words for the drawings on the page. He always gives me a thumbs-up and a big smile when I remember the words correctly. Yesterday, he gave me a big basket of hot french fries because I told him, "Good afternoon, Marvin. How are you? I would like a hamburger and Coke, please. It's hot today, yes?" You won't understand that, but I'll teach you!

I've drawn you a map of Prima Benita's house. It's a bit smaller than our house in Santa Clara. The room I share with Alejandro is just down the hall from the kitchen. The front yard doesn't have mango trees, but it does have a poinciana tree like we have in Cuba. I stare at the orange flowers a lot.

How are Mami and Papi? Abuelo and Abuela?

All the tíos and tías? So many faces and so many names. You all are so far away. Are you still on a break from school? Lucky if you are. I have to start school here in the United States in six weeks. The thought of that makes me want to vomit up the oatmeal Prima Benita serves for breakfast.

When you come to the United States, Pepito, don't eat the oatmeal.

Your brother,
Cumba

The music coming from the radio in Prima Benita's kitchen drifts down the hallway. She borrowed Alejandro's shortwave radio and tuned it to a station from Havana. I tap my finger to the rhythm, the swirling notes and light beat pulling me from concentrating on the English in the Flash Gordon comic book I'm trying to read, which might as well be written backward, upside-down, and in French. I close my eyes as a clarinet dances into the melody, picturing Papi lifting his shoulders and breathing deeply as he plays.

The song stops, and I sigh. The music changes, and my breath catches in my throat. I clench my fists, crumpling a page of the comic in my hands.

The edges of the paper cut my fingers as the trumpets and horns march down the hallway and pierce my ears.

"La Bayamesa," the Cuban national anthem.

I open my eyes and stare at the wall, not wanting to close them. I know if I do, I'll see the old man at the prison. I'll hear his voice rising above the wall. I'll feel the cracks of the rifles in my chest.

Heavy boots march down the hallway, and I grasp the paper in my hand tighter, smashing it into a tight ball. The doorknob turns, and I wait for Ignacio to burst through the door, spitting tobacco juice at me as he drags me off to the garrison.

"Niño, what are you doing to your book?" Prima Benita asks.

I shake my head, flinging the dark thoughts across the room. I smooth out the paper as best as I can and shove the comic under my pillow.

"Get Valeria for breakfast, please," she says.

That's right. I forgot. There's a girl in Prima Benita's house.

She arrived last night, one hand clasped around her gray suitcase, the other rubbing a gold ring hung from a chain around her neck. It reminded me of Mami, how she constantly worried the cross around her neck.

Prima Benita introduced her as Valeria from Havana. Alejandro gave her his usual scowl, which surprised me. They look like they're the same age. I thought he didn't want to hang out with me because I was so much younger. Every morning, he stomps up the street after breakfast and doesn't return until dinner.

After an awkward introduction—which consisted of the three of us just staring at one another—Prima Benita ushered Valeria to her new bedroom. I pretended not to hear the soft sobs coming through the wall, just as I'm sure Alejandro had to ignore my sniffles into my pillow the first week I was here.

It's embarrassing.

I tap softly on her door. "Valeria? Prima Benita says breakfast is ready," I call through the wood.

I hear a shuffling inside, and Valeria opens the door. Her dark brown hair hangs straight over her shoulders. She takes the gold ring hanging from her neck and tucks it into the neckline of her dress. The green plaid material and her long brown hair remind me of Adelita, the little girl who grasped my hand as we flew across the sea. The look of fear and nervousness in Valeria's eyes reminds me of Adelita the most. It doesn't look like she slept a minute last night.

"Gracias, Cumba," she says, giving me a half smile.

I clear my throat. "Prima Benita will tell you to speak English from now on."

Her smile grows a little wider. "Thank you, Cumba," she enunciates clearly.

We head down the hall to the kitchen. Valeria, Alejandro, and I sit at the kitchen table, our bowls of oatmeal steaming in front of us. I nudge the brown sugar bowl over to Valeria and hold up four fingers. She raises an eyebrow.

"Trust me," I whisper.

Prima Benita reads from her Bible again while we eat, first from the English column and then from the Spanish one. I find myself able to catch more words than before, mostly because Prima Benita always reads at a slow pace, clearly pronouncing each word. I smile when she reads the Spanish column, her voice sounding just like Abuela's.

I watch Valeria's face as she tastes her oatmeal for the first time. Her eyebrows scrunch up, and she swallows hard. If she's like me, she'd give anything for a guava pastelito right now. She gives me a wink as I slide the brown sugar bowl to her again.

After we finish, we wash our bowls and place them next to the sink to dry. Prima Benita gives us our spending money from the green cracker tin, and Alejandro storms out the door the second the coins hit his hand. I hold out my quarters in my palm to Valeria and tell her in English, "Two quarters. Twenty-five cents each."

She smiles as she drops the coins into the pocket of her dress.

Prima Benita passes me a piece of paper across the table. "I have your map for you," she tells me, pointing to the paper with black lines drawn on it.

Last night, I told Prima Benita about Adelita, mostly because Valeria reminded me of her so much. I asked if there was a way to find out where she went. Prima Benita told me that she was most likely under the care of the Catholic Welfare Bureau, given the nun that carted her off in the airport.

The lines on the map will lead me to their office in Miami.

Heading out of the house, I spy Valeria a few steps behind. "You can come with me, if you want," I tell her.

She shuffles next to me, and we head down the street.

I tell Valeria about my plan to find out about Adelita, but I can tell she's only half listening. She removes the gold chain with the ring from the neck of her dress and rubs it between her fingers. Each time we get to the end of a block, her head snaps in each direction. I know she's not looking for passing cars. She's looking for soldiers.

We take a bus downtown, something easily accomplished regardless of language. Just watch for the number you need and smile at the bus driver when you deposit your fare. Valeria presses her nose to the window as we roll past buildings, stores, and billboards.

"I've never seen so many stores," she whispers. Her hand still rests around her ring necklace, but her shoulders are no longer hunched with fear. She sits a little taller as she looks at the billboards advertising Coke, sunscreen, bread, coffee . . . you name it. I still can't understand most of the words on the ads, but they're pretty self-explanatory.

Buy me, they all say.

Following Prima Benita's map, I rub my thumb over the street name where we're supposed to get off the bus. I have no idea how it's pronounced. It would be a lot easier if it were a number.

The driver calls out a name in English, and Valeria nudges me. "He said the one we want," she tells me.

We walk down the street, following Prima Benita's map, stopping at a large concrete building at the corner. It looks more modern than most of the buildings in Santa Clara with their columns and scrollwork along the roof. This building is all right angles. I match the words CATHOLIC WELFARE BUREAU on a sign with the words on the map.

Reality hits me as we head toward the building. How exactly am I going to ask about Adelita if no one in this entire office speaks Spanish? My hand rests on the metal bar across the front door. This was a bad idea. We came all this way just to give the people inside blank stares as they spout nonsense we can't understand, the sounds swirling together into a fog.

I feel a hand on my back. "C'mon, Cumba. Let's find out about your friend," Valeria says next to me. She pushes into the building, and I follow her.

A large room is filled with desks and the sound of typewriters and people shuffling around. Some are dressed as nuns in habits of light blue and white, others wear priests' collars. And others are dressed like regular folks. They're all talking to one another in words I can't understand.

I look at Valeria. The signs hanging in the building might as well be written in German. I can make out only a few words, most of those being *the*.

A nun walks up to us. We must look like fools,

standing in the middle of the building, staring. She says something in English, her bright blue eyes smiling at us. That should make me feel more at ease, but I can't understand her.

She speaks again, a little slower this time, and thankfully not any louder. I fold and unfold the map in my hands, unsure of what to do. Just as I'm about to turn on my heels and bolt from the building, Valeria speaks next to me.

In English.

I hear her say "Adelita," and the nun smiles again. She puts her hand on my shoulder and points to a desk in the far corner of the room. As we follow the nun, Valeria gives me a wink.

The nun sits behind a desk and looks me in the eyes. Blond hair peeks out from under her habit. "What is your name?" she asks.

My chest deflates with relief. This I understand. "Cumba Fernandez," I tell her.

"I'm Valeria Rosales," Valeria says, sitting next to me in a wooden chair.

"I'm Sister Anne," the nun says. She smiles at me again. I sit back in my chair.

Sister Anne says something to Valeria in English, and she responds. They talk to each other for a few minutes. I try to make out what they're saying, scrunching my eyebrows together, as if that helps. But it's no use; they sound like they're talking underwater.

Sister Anne goes to a file cabinet behind her desk and ruffles through several papers. She takes out a file and places it on her desk. Running her long finger down a page in the file, she squints and leans closer to the page.

"Adelita Inés Morales Gonzales?" Sister Anne looks up at me.

I nod. I know Adelita's full name only because I read it on the luggage tag on her suitcase. It was written in careful letters, by a mami nervous about sending her child alone to a foreign country.

Sister Anne closes the file. "She is in Lincoln, Nebraska," she tells us.

I've never heard of that place. "What is Nebraska?" I ask.

Sister Anne holds up a finger and rises from behind the desk. She walks across the large room and out of our sight.

While she's gone, Valeria grabs the folder from the desk and opens it. She reads the papers inside.

"What are you doing?" I ask, looking behind me for Sister Anne.

"Just checking for a name," she says. I notice that she's rubbing her ring necklace again as she scans the page. Her eyes reach the bottom, and she sighs, closing the folder. She pushes it back across Sister Anne's desk.

"Who were you looking for?"

Valeria grips the ring on her necklace so tightly the veins in her hand look like they might pop through her skin. "No one," she sighs. "He's not there."

I'm about to ask her who "he" is when Sister Anne returns with a large book. It says ATLAS across the front. Thankfully, that word is the same in English as it is in Spanish. Sister Anne has brought a book of maps.

She thumbs through several pages and finally gets to the page she needs. She spreads her palm across it, smoothing the page down. She turns the book to us, and I recognize it as a map of the United States.

Pointing to the center of the map, she says, "Nebraska."

I raise my eyebrow. I look from Miami, Florida, to Sister Anne's finger next to Lincoln, Nebraska. It's so far away!

I think of the question I want to ask, roll it around in my head, and practice it a few times. Finally, I say, "She go airplane to Nebraska?"

"No, she went on a train," Sister Anne replies. I

look closer at the map, over all the different colored states between Florida and Nebraska. The United States is enormous.

Valeria and Sister Anne start speaking to each other again, but I'm too busy tracing my finger from Florida to Nebraska to try to understand. I picture little Adelita sitting on an unfamiliar train, passing rivers, mountains, and plains she's never seen before. Did she find someone's hand to hold as the train left the station? Did someone help put her suitcase above her seat?

Valeria turns to me and explains her conversation with Sister Anne. "She says that Adelita arrived in Lincoln, Nebraska, two weeks ago and is living with a family there. She'll stay until her family can come from Cuba, just like we're staying with Prima Benita. The Catholic Church has sent kids to Delaware, Indiana, and New Mexico, too." Valeria points to each state on the map as she explains. They're all very far away from Cuba.

I look at Sister Anne sitting behind her desk, her hands folded in her lap. "Thank you," I tell her. I want to tell her more. I want to tell her that Adelita liked the Coke they served on the airplane but that she didn't like the salty peanuts. I want to tell her that Adelita was worried her mother wouldn't know where she finally settled. I want to ask her if they speak Spanish in Nebraska.

But I can't. So I just repeat, "Thank you."

Sister Anne smiles at us and gets up from her chair. She walks us to the front of the building, a hand on each of our shoulders. I stick out my hand and thank her again. She takes my hand in hers and says, "Bless you, child. Bless you."

Behind her shoulder, I look down a narrow, dimly lit hallway. There's a long wooden bench perched outside an office. A boy sits on the bench, his head in his hands, his black hair fallen over his face. The boy sits up and shakes his hair out of his face. His eyes are rimmed red, and his cheeks are stained with tears.

As Valeria pushes me out the front entrance of the building, the boy looks at me.

It's Alejandro.

He stands up quickly and rushes down the hallway. Before I can say anything, Valeria leads me out into the bright Miami sun.

CHAPTER 15

Querido Cumba,

How are you, big brother? Mami gave me a stamp so I can write to you. I had to go back to school last week. They made me wear a uniform, too. I don't like it. The red shorts make me look like Abuela dressed me up for Christmas, and the blue bandanna is always hot on my neck. I change the second I come home.

We're not allowed to go to church anymore. After Fidel kicked out all the yuma priests, he closed all the churches, too. Abuela still reads her Bible to me in the kitchen. She says God is in our kitchen just as much as He's in church. I wonder if He likes café con leche.

You've been gone two months, and we miss you. I'm not supposed to tell you this, but Mami sits in our room sometimes. She holds one of your model airplanes, the P-51, I think. She pretends I don't notice that she's been crying. Papi's songs on his clarinet sound a little bit sadder, a little bit slower. But I shouldn't tell you this.

So what is the big United States like? Have you seen cowboys have a gunfight yet? What is school like there? Are the priests nice, or do they make you memorize the order of popes from since forever? That's too many questions.

I'm going to end this letter by saying see you soon so it will come true.

Your little brother... Wait, am I still a little brother if you aren't in the house anymore? Never mind.

Pepito

When I was seven, we took a trip to Caibarién on the north shore. I built a sandcastle for Pepito. Since he was only two, he tried to eat the tower with his pudgy hands. Mami brought guava-and-cheese sandwiches for us to snack on while Papi and Abuelo fished from the shore.

I spent hours in the water lying on my back, letting the waves lift me up and down. I closed my eyes from the bright sun as the sea rocked me. When I opened my eyes, I was much farther from the shore than I imagined. I could see Mami waving her arm, Pepito on her hip, telling me to come in.

The water before me looked calm, eerily flat. Swimming to shore should be easy. I started to kick my legs, but it was as if some creature underwater was holding them back. I could hear Papi and Abuelo shouting from the shore, pointing at something I couldn't see.

The seawater splashed in my eyes, stinging them. I blinked, scratching the corner of my eyes with salt. A large wave slammed into me, pummeling me to the bottom. I gasped, sucking in salt water, burning my throat. I pushed my legs on the sandy seafloor and choked in air at the surface.

Papi and Abuelo continued waving and shouting from the shore. Another wave slapped me and pulled at my legs. The muscles in my arms felt heavy from trying to swim to the shore. I looked again with burning eyes at Papi and Abuelo and saw them telling me to swim along the shore instead of toward it.

I slapped the surface of the water with my arms and pushed through the waves. Eventually I made it out of the riptide and onto the shore. My chest heaved, each breath on fire from the salt water. My hands clawed the sand as I coughed, my legs giving out and throwing me to the sandy ground. Abuelo slapped my back, and Papi threw a towel around me as Mami brushed my wet hair from my forehead.

That was the day the sea almost sucked me in, drowning me in its salty waves.

And that's the memory that swirls to the front of my brain as I stand before my new American school.

The large wooden doors of Ponce de León Junior High School creak as I climb the front steps and open them. "Uuuh-oooh," they seem to mutter.

I recognize the name of my new school. Ponce de León was a Spanish explorer in the 1500s. Padre Tomás said that while lots of people think he searched all over Florida for the Fountain of Youth, that's not really true. He was driven out by the Calusa people, who were living in Florida. So my school is named after a man searching for something he'd never find, thrown out by people who didn't want him there.

Perfect.

I'm by myself on my first day. Since they're older, Valeria and Alejandro go to Coral Gables High School. I would say they at least have each other, but I'm not sure how much support Alejandro will be.

The first wave that hits me when I cross the

threshold is noise. Students shouting, bells ringing, lockers slamming. I'm caught up in a wave of kids moving down the hall. I try to catch my breath and calm myself, but the noise swirls around me. And I don't understand any of it.

My schedule is in my hand. I'm afraid the sweat from my palms has smudged the list of classes, teachers, and rooms. I can understand most of what's on the paper. The school subjects aren't that much different from Spanish. Historia, matemáticas, geografía, ciencias. I can read the room numbers, too. But finding the actual classrooms in this sea of students and winding halls is another story. My head already hurts.

I look at my schedule as I'm pushed down the hallway, the wave of noise building and crashing against the concrete walls. I glance at room numbers and finally find the one I need. I need to swim upstream only a little before I fall into the room. My stomping feet as I catch myself echo in the classroom. There's a desk at the front of the room, and behind it sits a man wedged into his chair, his generous stomach pouring over the armrests.

There are a few students in the classroom and a few open desks. From what I can tell, I'm the only Cuban in the class. I'm not sure where to sit, so I walk up to the teacher. My schedule says he's Mr. McLaughlin, but I can't even begin to guess how that's pronounced. Mr. McLaughlin is hiding behind a newspaper and doesn't see me approach. I clear my throat. I hear a grunt from behind the newspaper, and Mr. McLaughlin lowers it to look at me. His round face and curly red hair remind me of a glasseye snapper that Abuelo once caught. He'd tossed it back into the waves, saying it wasn't any good.

I hold out my schedule to Mr. McLaughlin. He doesn't even look at it and simply waves his hand at the desks in the classroom with another grunt. He mumbles something in English. I want to tell him that I'm a new student. That I'm nervous. I want to ask him where I should sit. I can't hear any of my lessons at Royal Castle with Marvin over the thudding of my heartbeat in my ears. All I can remember is the question that Prima Benita made me practice over and over at breakfast this morning. She said it would be my most important phrase to know at school.

"May I go to the bathroom?"

I briefly consider asking Mr. McLaughlin this and retreating from the classroom back into the current of noise and nonsense.

Mr. McLaughlin mumbles again in English and points to an empty desk in the front row. I tuck my schedule into my pocket and shuffle my way to the desk.

A loud bell rings in the classroom, and I jump. Mr. McLaughlin groans, sets his paper aside, and opens a green notebook on his desk. He begins reading names. The student next to me says, "Here." A student behind me says the same thing after Mr. McLaughlin says something. I grip the corners of my desk, leaning in and straining to hear Mr. McLaughlin say my name. I go over in my mind exactly how I'm going to pronounce *here*. But then Mr. McLaughlin calls another name, and a kid sitting in the back of the classroom says something that starts with a *p*. He calls another name, and that student says the same thing. My stomach starts to twist. What am I supposed to say? I assume Mr. McLaughlin's list is alphabetical. Surely he's getting close to my name.

He grunts again and pauses. He squints and holds his notebook closer to his stubby red nose. "Fern-an-days, Come-buh," he says.

I swallow hard and lift my hand. "Here," I say, willing my voice not to quiver.

Mr. McLaughlin grunts and continues with his

list. When he gets to the end, he points to a number written on the chalkboard. The students around me open the books on our desks, so I do the same. I assume the number on the board is the page we're supposed to turn to, so I flip in my book to page 173.

I scan the sparse classroom. There's a map of the United States on the bulletin board near the door, but that's the only decoration. Above the chalkboard hangs a plaque that says NEW YORK CITY POLICE DEPARTMENT. Do schools in the United States use policemen as teachers? I shake my head, hoping the confusion will fly from my ears.

Mr. McLaughlin grunts and points to the girl in the front row opposite me. She begins to read from page 173. I press my index finger to the page and try to follow along.

After two paragraphs, Mr. McLaughlin grunts from behind his newspaper. "Next," and another student in the front row starts reading.

Santa María, save me. He's making us all read out loud. Sweat starts to prickle my forehead. My finger sticks to the page as I try to follow along with the next student. She's reading quickly, and it's all I can do to pick out words I recognize and match them to the page.

"Next," Mr. McLaughlin barks after two

paragraphs. At any moment, I expect him to lower the newspaper, revealing Ignacio's greasy beard chomping on a cigar. My stomach starts to roll, and I swallow hard.

I scan the page. If he's having each student read two paragraphs and there are two more students to go before me . . . I look ahead to the paragraph I'll have to read when it's my turn. I squint at the words. I'm pretty sure I can sound some of them out, but I have no idea what they mean.

"Next."

I'm so focused on trying to find where my turn in the reading will be I've completely lost place with the class.

A boy in the front row mumbles as he reads in a low voice, making it impossible to understand what he's saying. My foot starts to fidget in time with the waves of nausea in my stomach. I look at the text-book of the student sitting next to me, but she's not following along with her finger like I am.

"Next."

The girl beside me turns a page along with the rest of the class. Okay, that means we're at the top of this new page. The girl begins to read. I follow along again with my index finger, tracing the bottoms of the words while keeping my eye on the paragraph I'm supposed to start on.

"Next."

My heart jumps into my throat. I glance at Mr. McLaughlin, hoping he'll take pity on the new kid, but his face is buried behind his newspaper. He doesn't even see me.

I clear my throat, trying to shove my heart back down. I look at the first sentence in my paragraph.

"Lincoln was . . . elected president of the United States in the . . . fall . . . election of . . . one eight six zero."

I hear giggles erupt behind me.

I dig my fingernails into my thigh. My mouth feels dry, and I lick my lips. I continue. "The South was . . . chall—"

"Next."

My cheeks burn with embarrassment as the student behind me begins to read, floating quickly over each word with ease.

I don't try to follow along anymore. Student after student in the rows behind me read, their unintelligible words washing over me.

The bell on the wall rings, announcing the end of class. Everyone slams their textbooks shut, and I do the same. Filing out of the room with the rest of the class, I look back at Mr. McLaughlin, his red curly hair peeking out from behind his newspaper. He doesn't even look at me.

I'm carried into the hallway again and caught up in shuffling feet and knocking elbows. The waves carry me to math class, beat me against rocks in science class, and pull me under in English class.

I gasp for breath, waving my arms, begging someone, anyone, to understand me. My neck aches from tilting my head, trying to understand, as if one ear is more accustomed to English than the other.

The final bell of the day sounds, a nail slamming into my brain. I run from the school building and down the street. I close my eyes as I pass billboards I can't understand. Cars drive down the street, blaring music whose words I don't know.

No more. No more.

I reach Prima Benita's and race into my room, slamming the door shut. Shoving my hand into my pocket, I take out the caja de muertos domino and launch it across the room. It slams against the wall and falls to the floor. I sit on my bed in the darkness, head lowered, hands clenched against my ears, willing the noise to stop, begging the waves to quit beating and battering me, longing for someone to drag me to shore.

CHAPTER 16

Querido Cumba,

Abuelo and I planted bromeliads in the backyard all day today instead of going to church. Well, nobody went to church. Fidel says we can't. I know I complained whenever Mami made us go, but now I miss it. And I miss you. Write me.

Pepito

Querido Cumba que le echo de menos,

There are three fewer students in my class. Makes it hard to have a whole baseball team. I think they went to the United States. I asked Mami when I get to go. She just said to go clean my room. Why aren't you writing to me? Are you okay?

Your brother (remember me?),
Pepito

Querido Cumba,

I don't want to eat beans and rice anymore. I know Fidel will kick me out of Cuba for saying that (I wish!). Mami lost our ration book, and we haven't had meat all week. I'm going to hunt down a pig with Abuelo's machete. Do you have to eat beans and rice in the United States? Do you remember what that is? Do you remember Cuba? Do you remember us?

Pepito

Cumba,

Mami is worried. You need to write us.

Pepito

Mi hermano Cumba,

Soldiers came today and asked Papi questions. I hid under your old bed.

   Why aren't you writing?

Pepito

Cumba,

Abuelo says I have to put all these letters together in one envelope because we don't have enough stamps. So here you go. A bunch of letters from your long-lost brother, Pepito. I have brown eyes. I'm short. I can climb a tree better than you. Remember me?

Pepito

Dear Pepito,

I'm sorry I haven't written in two weeks. I hope Mami wasn't worried. After being at school all day, the last thing I could bring myself to do was write, even in Spanish. Prima Benita thinks I've been sick because I come home from school and sleep. School is so loud, so noisy with so much I can't understand,

I just need it to be quiet.

School is a hurricane of noise. Remember when that storm came through when you were little and the branches of the banyan tree banged on the windows all night? We couldn't sleep. That's school. It's all banging, all noise. I watch everyone's moves, to see what they're doing and guess if that's what I should be doing, too. The girls look at me and whisper to one another, giggling. I'm not sure I want to know what they're saying. The boys shout and push, like fighting roosters. I take back every bad thing I ever said about Padre Tomás. If I ever see him again, I'm going to hug him and buy him a mango batido.

How are Mami and Papi? Abuelo and Abuela? Take extra special care of them, Pepito. You're the big brother in the house now. Keep Demonio away from Mami. Pick up the mangos that fall from the tree for Abuela before they rot. Make sure Papi and Abuelo always have a plate of guava and cheese after dinner. That's their favorite, you know. Memorize Mami's smile. Record Papi's laugh.

I wish I had.

Still your big brother,
Cumba

It took me three tries to write that letter to Pepito. My hand hovered over the blank paper for an hour as I tried to decide what to say. It's hard to write to him. Having to send him a letter only reminds me that he's far away. I can't wander into the kitchen and catch him stealing Aracelia's cookies. I can't watch him sneak candy to Demonio as we walk home from school.

I can't.

I pick up the caja de muertos sitting on my desk and shove it into my pocket. I close my eyes as the air conditioner clicks on and whirs. All I hear is Ignacio's menacing chuckle, and my skin crawls.

Alejandro stomps into our room as I fold up my letter. He throws two books onto his bed and sits down with a huff. He grabs the small radio on the dresser between our beds and fiddles with the nobs. The sound of WGBC radio, an English news station, fills the room.

I want to ask him to turn it off. I want to beg him for no more noise. My brain can't handle it any-more. I put my hands over my ears and lay my head down on the desk, breathing slowly. I roll my ankles. They pop as my feet ache. These past two weeks, I've taken a different route to school each morning. Some are longer than others, and my shoes have given me angry blisters.

But soldiers can't follow you if you always go a different way.

I hear Alejandro get up and open a dresser drawer. Coins drop on the desk beside my head, the sharp sound like needle pricks in my brain.

"Explain," Alejandro says above me.

I look at the white gym sock filled with money that he put on the desk.

"I said explain. There are more coins in here than there should be. I think you know why."

I haven't known Alejandro long, but I know he mostly speaks in grunts and groans. This is the most he's ever said to me. And, of course, he still sounds angry when he's actually speaking.

I shrug, too tired to make my brain form sentences yet, in English or Spanish. I take a deep breath, deciding I should just come clean to Alejandro so this conversation will be over and I can slip into a coma.

"Prima Benita mixed up some of our clothes last week. So I was putting your shirt in your drawer when I saw the sock with the coins and the little girl's picture. She's your sister, right?"

Alejandro nods, his dark eyes still narrowed at me.

The moment I saw the picture of a girl about Pepito's age, standing on the beach with her long brown braids blowing in the wind, I thought of my own brother far away.

"I figured maybe you were saving up to get her something or help her. I don't know. I don't really need all the allowance Prima Benita has been giving us. School lunch is cheap. And gross. And there's not really anything I want. I thought you could use it more than me."

"I don't need help. I don't need charity," Alejandro says.

I want to put my head down on the desk. I don't want to argue. "So? Keep the coins, don't keep the coins. I don't care. I just thought it was the right thing to do."

Alejandro sits down on his bed and brushes his hair from his forehead, revealing the angry red scar that runs from his temple. "I know you saw me that day. At the Catholic Welfare Bureau office."

I rub my sweaty palms on my pant legs. "I . . . I was looking for information about a friend I met when I came over," I stammer. "I didn't know you'd be there."

"You never said anything."

I shrug. It feels like a lifetime ago when Valeria and I went to check on Adelita even though it's only been two months. Time is a blur of confusing

English words and homesickness. "It's none of my business."

Reaching under his bed, Alejandro grabs a base-ball. He takes a deep breath and smiles. At least, I think he does. I've never seen him smile before, so I can't be sure if he's just having a seizure.

"I'm looking for my sister. I've been saving up in case I need to pay for documents or anything."

"Where is she?" I ask.

Alejandro doesn't answer right away. At first, I think he hasn't heard me. The air conditioner perched in our window kicks on with a click and a whir. Cool air fills the room. Alejandro rubs his eyes and takes a deep breath.

"I don't know," Alejandro finally says. "That's what I was trying to figure out at the office that day."

He pounds his fist on his leg, and I jump. "I lost her. We were at the airport in Havana, and the guards detained her, said her papers were wrong. There's no way they could've been. I tried to stop them, and this guard hit me with the butt of his rifle. The next thing I know, I'm on the plane here."

I look at the scar on his temple, and he brushes his hair in front of it.

"A priest sitting next to me on the plane said he helped me on there, but he didn't see my sister," he continues. "I don't know if Marisol made it here or if she's still in Cuba."

"Can you write your parents and ask? That would be the first thing I would do if something happened to my brother."

Alejandro sighs and clenches his fists. "It's just me and Marisol. I lost Papi to Batista, and Mami to Fidel."

I stare at the veins popping out of his hands. He looks me in the eye and launches the baseball he's gripping into the corner of our room. It lands with a hard thud, and I jump.

"I hate Fidel," he mutters.

The air conditioner clicks off, and we sit in silence. I don't know what to say. How do you tell someone who's drowning that you don't have a life raft? How do you help someone who's starving if you don't have any food of your own?

I reach under the pillow on my bed and pull out my photograph of Papi, Mami, and my little brother, handing it to Alejandro. "I have Pepito," I tell him. "Every time I look at this picture, I can see him aiming his plastic cowboy gun at all the lizards, iguanas, and cats in our neighborhood."

"Marisol." Alejandro's voice catches on the name. "My sister, Marisol, probably would yell at him not to do that. And then she'd take in all the cats."

I chuckle.

Alejandro hands the photo back to me and sighs. "So school's been that bad?"

I groan and sit down.

"Yeah, I thought so," Alejandro says, stretching his arms behind his head and lying down on his bed. "You had me a little worried these past two weeks, you know? Thought maybe you were possessed by the spirit of Fidel or something. That one day I'd wake up and find 'hasta la victoria, siempre' scrawled all over the walls in cat blood."

Alejandro chuckles at his own joke. I just stare at him, unsure of what to say. This is the longest conversation we've ever had.

Hopping up and grabbing the baseball from the corner of the room, Alejandro tosses it at me, but I'm not ready. I can't raise my arms in time, and it bounces off my fingertips, thudding to the floor and rolling back to Alejandro's feet.

"Are you sure you're really Cuban?" he asks. "I'm pretty sure you're not allowed to be Cuban if you can't play baseball."

I give him a weak smile. "My papi and abuelo

were more into music than sports. I just like building things."

Alejandro nods and tosses the baseball up and down in his hand. He looks at me with his dark eyes and searches my face. He slowly throws the ball to me again, and this time, by some miracle, I catch it. I try to toss the ball up and down in my hand like Alejandro did, but I end up jamming my index finger with one throw and having to catch the ball in my other hand.

I chuckle. "Wanna teach me how to catch in the backyard?"

I may be pressing my luck with Alejandro, but the fresh air outside might help the noise of school blow away from my brain.

Alejandro smiles. "We can't let these Americans think we're not good at baseball. I suppose I have to. Can't let you give all of us a bad name."

As we walk down the hall, I take one look back in our room, Marisol's and Pepito's pictures perched side by side on the dresser.

CHAPTER 17

Dear Pepito,

These are the English words I've learned at school
so far. Pay attention. You'll hear these a lot when
you come over.

Be quiet.

Sit down.

Shut up.

Move.

Silence.

Listen.

Quiet down.

I'm trying to speak as much English as I can, but
all my teachers want me to do is be quiet.

I'm the only Cuban in my school. This means I'm
The Cuban Ambassador. All my teachers want me to
tell the class about Cuba. "Talk about Cuba, Cumba."
"Tell us about Cuba." I don't have the English to

tell them about Cuba. And what am I supposed to say? I don't think any of the kids in my class would be able to tell me about ALL of the United States. But they look at me and think every little thing I do is what all Cubans do. You know how I like to eat mango and cream cheese? I brought that for lunch one day. Now everyone thinks that's what all Cubans eat for lunch. I did really well on a math quiz we had last week. So guess what? All Cubans are good at math, evidently. I'm really tempted to wear my clothes backward and walk on my hands down the school hallways. I can just tell them, "That's what Cubans do."

Give Mami, Papi, Abuelo, and Abuela big hugs for me. And don't feed Demonio any candy!

Your Cuban Ambassador,
Cumba

After school, Alejandro and I throw his worn baseball around in Prima Benita's backyard. Alejandro already had a glove, and Prima Benita found another one for me in her attic. It's a little too big, but with my lack of skill, it doesn't make much of a difference.

My headaches after school aren't as bad anymore.

The rhythmic thud of the baseball in our gloves helps me think about something other than the drone of school noise.

"That's seventy-two," Alejandro says as he launches the ball at my glove. He makes me throw one hundred good pitches every day after school. I think it helps him get his mind off Marisol. Ever since our talk, he's smiled more and scowled less. But every so often, his eyes darken and he stares at a wall. I know he's thinking about who he left behind.

The same thing happens to me.

"Are you guys trying out for an American baseball team?" Valeria asks us as she sits down on the back steps of Prima Benita's house. She smooths out her blue skirt and lifts her hand to shield the setting sun from her eyes.

Alejandro chuckles. "Of course. But I think I'll try out for the team at school first."

"I'm just trying not to take a pitch to the nose," I tell her.

She smiles. "You know these Americans think Fidel was some kind of baseball star?"

Alejandro drops his gloved hand and grips the baseball in the other. "Qué tontería. I'd strike out el jefe easy."

"Why do they think Fidel played baseball, other

than the fact they think all Cubans play baseball?" I ask, winking at Alejandro.

"Some American reporter wrote that Fidel had a tryout with the New York Yankees," Valeria explains. "But he never made the team."

Alejandro throws the ball to me, and it thuds in my glove. I trace my thumb on the ragged laces.

"Would've been nice if he had, yeah?"

Valeria and Alejandro nod. I lob the ball back to Alejandro. He misses, and the ball rolls under Prima Benita's bougainvillea bush. A familiar dark shadow shades Alejandro's eyes once again.

Three Cuban kids standing in the middle of the Catholic Welfare Bureau office don't draw much attention. Everyone is too busy at their desks. Valeria sees Sister Anne and waves. She comes over to us, the same smile on her face and glint in her eyes that made me feel so comfortable when I first met her.

I wish Adelita had Sister Anne pick her up from the airport instead of Sister Sourface.

Sister Anne takes us to her desk, and we cram wooden chairs around it.

"It's so good to see you again," she tells us. I smile.

I understand her a lot more than I did the last time we met.

She slides a bowl of strawberry candies across her desk to us. They're the same candies that Abuela would always take out of her housecoat pocket and give me when Mami wasn't looking. I swallow down the pang of homesickness in my stomach.

Alejandro grabs one and places another in his pocket.

"So what can I do for the three of you?" Sister Anne asks.

Valeria straightens up in her seat. "We need you to be our detective and find people for us."

Sister Anne's smile grows wide across her face. She claps her hands together. "I always wanted to be a detective. Who are we looking for?"

Alejandro crumples the red metallic candy wrapper between his fingers. He reaches into his pocket and pulls out the photo he showed me. Sliding it across the desk to Sister Anne, he says, "My sister, Marisol. She was supposed to come over when I did, but . . ." Alejandro drops his head and clenches his fists. "She couldn't. I don't know if she's here or if she's still in Cuba."

Alejandro's English is pretty good. Am I the only one who didn't pay attention in class? I stare at everyone's lips as they talk about Alejandro's sister. I can make out most of what they're saying, but every once in a while, they lose me.

Sister Anne writes down all the information Alejandro tells her. When she's done, she looks at Valeria expectantly. "And you? Who are you looking for?"

Valeria's fingers once again clench around her necklace. Her eyes dart at Alejandro and me. With a quivering voice, she says, "My husband."

What? A few words that I heard Abuela shout when Pepito and I surprised her with a fake rubber snake bounce around in my head.

Alejandro stares at Valeria, and Sister Anne arches her eyebrow so high I think it might disappear under her habit.

Sister Anne clears her throat. "Excuse me? Your husband? You look like you're barely out of high school."

Valeria looks down at her lap. "I'm seventeen."

Folding her fingers under her chin, Sister Anne leans back in her chair and waits for Valeria to speak.

Valeria starts talking so quickly I can barely make out what she's saying. I catch only a few words, but they don't do much to help me understand how a girl half Mami's age could have a husband.

Gripping the ring on her necklace as she speaks, Valeria finally finishes her explanation to Sister Anne. I shrug at Alejandro, hoping he understood what she was saying and will catch me up later.

Sister Anne spends a few moments writing on the paper in front of her. She looks up at me. "And you? Who do we need to find for you?"

I think for a moment, practicing my words in my head. "I no have a husband. I no have a sister."

Sister Anne smiles. "Who do you have?"

I want to tell her I have a little brother who likes to dress up like a cowboy. A mother who is more afraid of stray cats and dogs than she is of parading soldiers. A father who could calm a hurricane with the sound of his music. An abuela who fills my belly with guava pastelitos and love. An abuelo who can conquer any coconut tree in all of Cuba.

That's who I have.

I blink back hot tears that start to form in the corners of my eyes. "I have a brother. I have a mother and father. I have a grandmother and grandfather. They are in Cuba. They no are here."

Sister Anne asks me their names, and I give them. She adds them to her paper.

Alejandro, Valeria, and Sister Anne begin talking, but I'm too distracted by thoughts of my family to listen. The hard wood of the chair I'm sitting on makes my back ache. I want Abuela to rub it for me.

I'm pulled from my thoughts as Valeria and Alejandro rise from their chairs.

I guess we're leaving.

Valeria explains to me that Sister Anne wants us to come back in a few weeks to see if she's found out anything about our families.

As we head out the door, I think about the hamburger and Coke I promised Alejandro and Valeria.

I'm not sure they'll be able to take the bitter taste of homesickness out of my mouth.

CHAPTER 18

Dear Pepito,

What does the kitchen smell like when Abuela makes ajiaco? Is Mami's laugh more like a tocororo's call or the crash of a wave against the shore? What do Papi's fingers look like as he runs them over the keys on his clarinet? How fast can Abuelo climb a coconut tree?

   I don't remember. Tell me, Pepito. Tell me everything.

   Tell me about Cuba.

Your brother,
Cumba

Math class is my friend. The numbers speak words I can understand. No matter the country, no matter the language, I can count on them to behave the way I expect. No surprises.

My only surprise in math class is the kid who sits next to me. Ever since the first day of school three weeks ago, I've noticed he always pulls out a folded newspaper from underneath his math textbook when Mr. Gearhart isn't looking. It says *The Daily Racing Form* across the top. I'm not quite sure what that means, but there's a silhouette of running horses on either side of the words. Today he takes his pencil and circles numbers on the page, completing calculations in the margins just as much as he does Mr. Gearhart's problems in his notebook.

"Oh, this is a good one," he mumbles, licking his lips and circling something on the newspaper.

He catches me watching him and says something in English I don't quite understand. I stop biting my nails and shrug.

Mr. Gearhart is facing the board as he completes a problem, so the kid leans toward me and shows me the newspaper. "This one. Toasted Butter. Good horse," he says, giving me a thumbs-up.

I look at the newspaper. It's filled with page after page of numbers. There are a few words on it. I think they're the names of horses. This is my kind of newspaper.

"How you know good horse?" I whisper.

Mr. Gearhart turns around from the board and claps. "Boys. Listen," he says.

"Sorry, Mr. Gearhart," I say.

I feel a twinge of excitement. I just got in trouble for speaking English in class. Abuela would be furious with me, but I'm happy. This means I'm making progress.

Two girls behind me giggle and whisper. My cheeks turn red. I hear one say, "Sorry, Mr. Gearhart," mimicking my accent.

My feeling of excitement tumbles into my stomach. I look at the boy and watch him stick out his tongue at the girls. He holds up a finger, telling me to wait, and slides the newspaper back under his textbook.

We finish the problems quickly. At least, I do. Not only do I love numbers, but Padre Tomás has already taught me how to do this.

I look over and notice the boy isn't completing the problems with as much ease as I am. At one point, he even lowers his head on his desk and groans. I smile. He reminds me of Amaro. Any second, I expect him to see if he can balance his pencil on his nose.

As class ends, we're dismissed to lunch in the cafeteria, a wave of noise and bodies flooding down the hall. I've gotten in the habit of eating in the corner of the cafeteria, my back turned from all the other students. I need a break from all the noise. If I could eat outside, I would. Just to get away from all the words, all the shouts I don't understand. Maybe across the street, down the block, maybe all the way to Cuba.

I poke my fork at the mysterious glob on my tray. American food is weird. I file down the cafeteria line, no say in what I get to eat. The sour-looking lunch ladies, their hair secured in nets that remind me of when Abuelo went fishing in Camagüey, fling blobs of various shades of gray and brown onto my tray. In Santa Clara, I got to go home every day for lunch and eat Aracelia's cooking. My mouth starts to water at the thought of her food.

Someone slaps down a newspaper next to me on the table.

"So let me tell you about good horses," a voice says.

I look up and see the boy from math class. He sits down next to me and begins talking. He points to numbers in the newspaper and speaks quickly and excitedly.

"Slow down, please," I interrupt.

He smiles. The freckles on his nose wrinkle. I've

never seen so many freckles on someone's skin before. They dance across his face, burning stars in a pale galaxy.

"Okay. Good horses. This newspaper lists all the horses." The boy runs his finger down a page in the newspaper. There are names on the left side and a series of numbers after each name. I don't understand most of the names. The words are weird. But I pick out a few.

My Gallant Daisy.

New York Times.

Skipping Jupiter.

"What are the numbers?" I ask the boy, shoving my lunch tray aside.

The boy points to the top of the page. "This is the name of the race. See? This says Gulfstream. That's here in Miami."

I don't know the word *Gulfstream*, but I figure it might be the name of a place where they have horse races.

The boy points to a list of names under the word *Gulfstream*. "These are the horses. They race at Gulfstream Race Track."

I look up as a group of four boys walks past us. One of them points to me and sneers, "The blue shirt again. What a surprise."

The three boys with him cackle as another says, "Let me guess. Green shirt tomorrow?"

Heat floods my face, and I stare down at my tray as the boys laugh, slapping one another on the back and walking away.

I have only three shirts and two pairs of pants in my dresser drawer at Prima Benita's. That's all I came with from Cuba. I try to make sure I rotate what I wear, and Prima Benita ensures my clothes are always clean. I've considered asking Alejandro to share, but he's a foot taller than I am.

So it's blue shirt, green shirt, white shirt with either my black pants or my khaki pants. Every week. I have to be careful not to stain or get a hole in anything, or my options will be even worse. And I'd like to leave coming to school in just my underwear to my nightmares.

I grip my fork, embarrassment ruining my appetite.

"They're nose pickers, you know," I hear the boy next to me say.

I shrug, not quite sure what he's said.

"They pick their noses," the boy repeats, shoving his index finger into his nostril. "And they eat it!"

He sticks his finger right in front of his mouth and laughs.

I process what he's said, and a giggle bubbles up from my throat and pours out of my mouth. I smile, and the boy winks.

I nod at the newspaper the boy is holding, and he continues. "These numbers are information about the horse. The races they've run, if they won, how far the race was."

The boy doesn't react to the fact that I'm staring at his lips and scrunching my eyebrows, concentrating on his every word. He continues showing me all the numbers and explaining how he uses the numbers to figure out who the best horse in the race is.

I nod and smile. "You like horses?" I ask him.

The boy laughs. "I like horse races."

We look over the newspaper together as he points out the horses he likes. I realize I've been able to ignore the noise in the cafeteria as we talk.

"My name is Cumba," I tell him. "I am from Santa Clara, Cuba."

The boy smiles, revealing crooked teeth that Mami would click her tongue and shake her head at. "I'm Arnold. I'm from here."

After lunch, we clean up our trays and walk down the hall together, Arnold forming a freckled seawall between me and the jarring waves of voices and lockers.

CHAPTER 19

It's been three weeks since we visited Sister Anne. Three weeks of the drumming, nonsensical noise of school. Three weeks throwing the baseball in the backyard with Alejandro. Three weeks wondering how Valeria is married but Prima Benita is not.

My fingernails have started to grow a little since I don't dream about Ignacio as much anymore. His greasy beard is starting to fade from my memory, and I'm not searching for him around every corner as I walk to school. I can finally breathe the salty sea air without thinking of his sour sweat.

Alejandro, Valeria, and I wait at the bus stop after school. It's our day to go to the Catholic Welfare Bureau to check in with Sister Anne.

As we stand at the bus stop, I remember something Mr. Gearhart, my math teacher, said to me at the end of class. It confused me at the time. But almost everything does.

"Do you guys know what Yom Kippur is?"

Alejandro chuckles. "It happened to you, too?"

Valeria shakes her head and smiles as I look from her to Alejandro in confusion. "What do you mean?" I ask.

"Where'd you hear that, Cumba?" Valeria asks. "Did someone say 'Happy Yom Kippur' to you?"

I nod. "My math teacher."

Valeria smiles, and Alejandro raises his hand. "Us too," he tells me.

I scrunch my eyebrows together, confusion still plastered on my face.

Thankfully, Valeria explains. "There aren't a lot of Cubans in Miami. The blanquitos here think we're too white to fit what they think Cubans should look like, but we're still darker than all of them. So I guess they think we're Jewish?"

I bite my lip. "That makes about as much sense as a wool coat in Havana."

Alejandro tucks in his shirt as the bus arrives. "I don't think anyone would ever accuse these Americans of making sense." He smirks as he gets on the bus.

I settle in next to Valeria on the bus and watch her run her thumb along the smooth metal of her ring. I've been too embarrassed to ask her about her husband, but I decide to dive in.

"How did you get married?" I ask her, pointing at her necklace.

Valeria cocks her head to the side and looks at me with confusion.

I scuff my feet on the floor of the bus. "I didn't understand when you explained to Sister Anne. I'm still learning."

Patting me on the shoulder, Valeria says, "I met Fernando in school. We wanted to get married, but our parents said we were too young. I found out they were sending me to the United States a week before he was. So we got married the day before I left, and he gave me this ring. He was supposed to come right after me, but I don't know if he's here yet. I haven't gotten any letters from him."

I bite my lip, chewing on the words she's told me. "The not knowing is the hardest, I think."

Valeria nods. "Yes. Yes, it is."

The bus finally groans to a stop near the Catholic Welfare Bureau. Sister Anne rushes to greet us when we arrive. She grabs Alejandro by the arm and exclaims, "I found her! I found her!"

Alejandro nearly falls to his knees. Valeria and I have to help him walk to Sister Anne's desk. He's peppering her with questions, half in English, half in Spanish.

We sit down next to him, and Sister Anne places

her hand on his shoulder, standing in front of him.

"She's in the Everglades Refugee Camp for Cubans. She arrived two weeks after you did. We are working on bringing her here to Miami."

Alejandro collapses, and he places his head in his hands. Soft sobs shake his shoulders. Valeria rubs his back and smiles at me, tears brimming in her own eyes.

A victory for one of us is a victory for all of us.

The rest of our visit is a blur. Sister Anne doesn't have any information about Valeria's husband. I don't expect her to have any information about my family. I'm still getting regular letters from Pepito. They'll let me know if they're coming over.

We head to Royal Castle to celebrate Alejandro's good news. Marvin greets us with hamburgers and Cokes all around with a basket of fries to share. He knows our regular order.

"Why so happy today?" he asks, setting down our food as we slide into a booth.

"Alejandro sister is coming here," I tell him.

Marvin smiles and slaps Alejandro on the back. "Wonderful! Wonderful!" he exclaims, rushing behind the counter.

We dig into our dinner, and Marvin returns with

a large chocolate shake with three straws. "To celebrate. I'm very happy for you, young man. Family is important."

Marvin heads back to his post behind the counter, taking orders from the dinner rush. Valeria, Alejandro, and I chew in silence, basking in our victory.

A man sitting behind Valeria says something in a gruff voice that I don't understand. Alejandro turns, gives the man a sour look, and returns to eating his hamburger.

The man says something again, this time louder. I don't know what he's saying, but his voice has an edge to it that makes me uncomfortable.

"What's he saying?" I ask Valeria.

She rolls her eyes. "He says Cuba is ungrateful. He says we threw away everything with the revolution."

Alejandro tosses the other half of a french fry he bit onto the table. "I didn't realize we were sitting next to a foreign-policy expert."

"Speak English!" the man barks.

This I understand.

"Just ignore him," Valeria says, sliding the chocolate milkshake over to me.

Alejandro starts humming under his breath. It's a tune I know well. I start humming along, and

Alejandro winks at me. Valeria taps her fingers on the table.

"Guantanamera, guajira, guantanamera," she sings, her soft voice filling the restaurant.

Alejandro picks up a french fry and waves it around like a conductor. We join Valeria in singing along.

"Yo soy un hombre sincero, de donde crece la palma."

Marvin claps along to our song.

The man gets up, throws his food in the trash, and pushes his way out the door, grumbling the whole time.

"I guess he doesn't like good music," Marvin says, and sets another chocolate shake down on our table.

Today is a good day.

CHAPTER 20

Cumba,

You have to come back.

Mami and Papi are gone.

The soldiers came. I hid under your bed again. There was a lot of shouting and banging. When I crawled out from under your bed, they were gone.

I ran next door to Abuelo and Abuela's house. I'm staying with them now.

Abuelo says that Mami and Papi are being held for questioning. I'm not sure what that means. Why can't the soldiers just ask them questions at home? Why do they need to ask them questions at all? Did someone from the Committee whisper about them? Doña Teresa keeps trying to peek in our windows all the time.

Abuelo said not to tell you. Abuela said it wasn't good to make you worry.

But I have to tell you. So I stole a stamp.
I don't want to be alone anymore, hermano.
You need to come home.

Pepito

The tile floor of Prima Benita's kitchen is cold and hard. My tears puddle on the cream squares, and my hand slips when I push myself up into Prima Benita's arms. I can feel her hand rubbing on my back and her voice in my ear, whispering, "It's okay, niño. It's okay."

I'm not aware of much else.

Every time I close my eyes, hot tears drip down my cheeks, and I picture a green-fatigued Ignacio bursting into our house in Santa Clara, dragging Mami and Papi out with a sneer on his face.

Did Mami clutch her necklace as he pulled her away?

Did soldiers crumple Papi's linen suit when they grabbed him?

I want to put my arms around Pepito. I want to calm him down with a silly game of dominoes.

But I can't. I'm not there.

And deep down, when I root around in the corners of my heart, despite the strong voice in my head telling me to stay away, I wonder if all this is my fault.

Prima Benita grabs me by the arms with a soft grip and helps me into a chair. The cold metal sticks to the backs of my legs, and I shiver.

Pepito's letter is crumpled in my hands, the pencil marks smudged by my tears. I look it over again through watery eyes, reading and memorizing every word. Prima Benita's low voice drones on in the background, but I'm not listening to her. I'm reading about what I've done.

This is my fault.

This is all my fault.

Prima Benita puts her arm around me. "We can pray for them, niño. Let's pray."

She places her hands over mine on the kitchen table, but I draw them back and shove Pepito's letter into my pocket. "Pray? What good is that?"

I stand up, knocking my chair over. It smacks hard against the tile floor. I move toward my bedroom, but Prima Benita stands in front of me. "Cumba, it will be okay," she says, putting her hands on my shoulders.

I shrug off her grip and push past her. Throwing open the bedroom door, I reach under the bed and pull out my suitcase. I open my drawer in the dresser and shove my clothes inside.

Alejandro pops his head in the doorway. "Hey, what are you doing, Cumbito?"

I wipe the snot from my nose on the back of my hand. "Don't call me that."

I slam my suitcase shut and clutch it to my chest. "I'm going home. I shouldn't have come here. I've put everyone in danger. If anything happens to them, it'll be my fault."

Alejandro moves into our bedroom and sits down on my bed. "What happened?" he asks.

I set my suitcase back on the bed and pull Pepito's letter out of my pocket. The caja de muertos falls out with it and clanks to the floor.

"Here. I don't care if you read it," I say, holding the paper out to Alejandro. He takes it, and I watch his eyes scan the words as I gnaw on a fingernail.

I reach under the bed and pick up the caja de muertos. Proof of my bad luck. Proof that Fidel still has his claws in my back, even a hundred miles away.

When Alejandro finishes reading, he sighs and rests the letter on the bed. Standing slowly, he walks over to our dresser and grabs our gloves and baseball.

"We haven't done our hundred catches yet today. Let's go in the backyard," he says, holding my glove out to me.

I grab Pepito's letter off the bed and shove it into my pocket. "Are you crazy? I'm not playing baseball."

Tears start to well up again in my eyes. I hear Ignacio's growl rush in my ears, the same growl I heard as he towered above me in the hallway of our house in Santa Clara. Did he scare Pepito the same way?

Alejandro takes my hand and puts the baseball in it. "Cumba, what exactly were you planning to do once you packed your suitcase? Hijack a plane? Swim to Cuba? If you actually do manage to go back, what are you going to do? March right up to Fidel and slap him on his greasy beard and tell him you want your parents back?"

"Shut up!" I yell at Alejandro, throwing the baseball across the room. It slams into Alejandro's radio, crashing it to the floor and smashing it to pieces.

Alejandro takes a deep breath and brushes his hair from his eyes. The scar on his forehead is healing and doesn't look as angry as it usually does.

"Well, your aim is improving," he says, walking over and picking up the pieces of radio. He deposits them in the trash bin in our room as I sit down on my bed, head in my hands.

I close my eyes, trying to decide how long it

would take me to walk to the airport from Prima Benita's house.

"I know helpless, Cumba," Alejandro says next to me. "I know not being able to fix things, even though you really want to."

He grabs my arm and helps me stand. "Let's do our hundred catches. Maybe while we're throwing, we'll figure something out."

I wipe my tears and follow Alejandro out to the backyard, passing Prima Benita at the kitchen table, her hands folded and head bowed in prayer.

The snap of the baseball landing in our gloves as Alejandro and I throw the ball back and forth sounds too much like soldiers' boots, stomping on the dirt streets in front of my house in Santa Clara. I struggle to catch my breath as the ball grows heavier with each throw. Alejandro doesn't say anything. He pitches to me in silence, but every so often, I look at his lips and see him muttering, "Please, God. Please."

We pray as we toss the ball back and forth. We pray for family so far away. We pray for family we will never see. We pray for the strength to keep throwing as the world spins out of control.

CHAPTER 21

The rubber on the bottom of my shoes melts into the linoleum lining the hallway at school as I drag my feet. My chin presses to my chest, my head weighed down by heavy, dark thoughts. I slump in my seat in history class, my fists clenched as I block out the noise around me. The caja de muertos makes calluses on my palm, burning each time it rubs my skin. I croak out a "here" when Mr. McLaughlin mispronounces my name once again.

He grunts and points to the page number scrawled on the board as usual, and the students around me flip open their textbooks. I leave mine closed on my desk, knowing the words I'm supposed to read would get twisted in my mouth.

The words I want to read are lost, and I'm afraid they're gone forever. *Mami and Papi are home. They are safe.*

My eyelids droop as the class drones on reading

aloud. I didn't sleep last night. Every time I closed my eyes, I felt Ignacio's hot grip on my ankles, trying to yank me off the bed. My head pounded with the sound of his stomping boots.

It's my turn to read aloud from the textbook. I cross my arms. The boy sitting behind me nudges my shoulder, and I shake my head. Mr. McLaughlin doesn't even look from behind his newspaper.

"Next!" He grunts as giggles erupt from a corner of the classroom.

The boy behind me clears his throat and starts to read as I sink lower in my chair.

When the bell rings mercifully, I push my way out of the classroom, nearly knocking over the boy who was sitting behind me.

"I think he's broken," I hear him tell another student.

I trudge into the hallway, wanting to disappear into the sea of students.

It's usually hard enough to concentrate on a regular day at school. To dissect every word I hear, tumble it around in my brain, and try to put it back together so it makes sense. But when Ignacio is stomping in my brain and holding every word hostage, understanding anything is impossible.

I stare at the faces walking past me. After school,

they'll go home to their moms and dads, brothers and sisters. They'll climb into their beds and have dreams of cowboys, apple pie, and shopping malls, or whatever Americans dream about.

They won't have nightmares of shouting soldiers. Of the loud crack of rifles. Of shouts and screams.

A locker slams next to me, and I jump. I look ahead, and my breath catches in my throat.

He found me. I don't know how, but he found me.

There's a man with a thick black beard standing next to a classroom door in the hallway. He pulls on the collar of his green fatigue shirt. Scanning the sea of students, his black eyes fall on me, and he sneers, revealing crooked yellow teeth.

Ignacio. He's found me.

I stop in my tracks, and Arnold slams into my back, his head buried in *The Daily Racing Form*.

"Hey, Cumba," he says.

I barely hear him, my eyes still locked on Ignacio as my heart pounds in my ears. I open my mouth to explain, but nothing comes out, my words suffocated by my fear.

Pushing past Arnold, I run to the boys' bathroom across the hall and away from Ignacio.

Slamming the door open, I gasp as I try to catch my breath, sucking down the stale air.

Two boys in the bathroom stare at me as I grip the edges of the cold porcelain sink, muttering, "No puede ser, no puede ser."

It can't be. I don't know how he did it, but Ignacio found me.

"What a weirdo," I hear one of the boys say as they leave the bathroom.

No matter how hard I try, I can't unclench my fists from the bathroom sink, and my hands start to ache.

"Bad breakfast?" Arnold says as he enters the bathroom, tucking his newspaper into the back pocket of his pants.

I look at him in the mirror and shake my head. My chest still heaves as my frozen body tries to catch up with my racing breath.

"Whoa, Cumba. What's wrong?" Arnold asks, slowly approaching me.

I keep shaking my head, hoping to fling out the thoughts crushing my skull.

"The man," I gasp.

Arnold's eyebrows scrunch together. "Man? What man?"

"Man. He here for me."

Arnold bites his lip. "Cumba, I don't know what you're saying."

My hands come unglued from the sink and fly at Arnold, pushing his chest and tumbling him back against the bathroom wall.

"El hombre en el pasillo. Es Ignacio. Está aquí porque no fui a la guarnición. Está aquí para mi."

Arnold's mouth drops open as I let go of the front of his shirt. "Sorry, man. Now I really don't understand you," he says.

My legs give out, and I slump down the bathroom wall next to Arnold. I draw my knees to my chest and lower my head, my hands shaking.

Arnold steps over to the bathroom door and peeks out. "Are you talking about Mr. Mitchell? The guy with the black beard?"

I look up, the tears I tried to hold back spilling out and flooding my cheeks. I nod. "Sí. Ignacio."

Arnold closes the door and shrugs. "I don't know what Mr. Mitchell's first name is, but I'm pretty sure it's not Ignacio. He's just a teacher, Cumba."

I press my hands to the cold tile floor at my sides and take a deep breath. A loud bell rings, echoing in the bathroom and shouting at us to get to class. Arnold slides down the wall and sits next to me.

We sit in silence, my ears still ringing from the bell. Water drips from one of the faucets, a clock ticking off seconds. I feel a light touch on my fingers and look down to see Arnold's hand wrapped around mine.

I close my eyes and try to match my breath to Arnold's. It's nice that he doesn't ask me to explain. I don't have the words for it anyway. I don't have the words to explain that I thought a teacher was a Cuban soldier, stomping across the sea to drag me back to the island. I don't have the words to let Arnold know that I don't know what's happened to Mami and Papi.

All I can do is squeeze Arnold's hand. Because I don't have the words to tell him I'd sink through the floor without it.

CHAPTER 22

Dear Pepito,

Are Mami and Papi back? Are you still staying at
Abuelo and Abuela's? Please write back and let me
know what's going on.

I don't know what else to say.

Please write.

Cumba

"I have a plan, Cumba," Arnold says to me at the
beginning of math class.

"A plan for what?" I ask.

Arnold flashes me his latest test, a large red F
marked by Mr. Gearhart at the top.

"Mr. Gearhart, I need help," Arnold declares. Our
math teacher can't help but nod in agreement. "I
know I did bad on our test. I still don't get all this
geometry stuff."

Arnold waves his test in front of Mr. Gearhart's face. "How am I ever supposed to become a horse trainer if I can't pass math class? I'll confuse a one and three-sixteenths race with a mile and a half race and get fired."

I bite my lip, both amused at Arnold and jealous at how easily he talks about the future and what he wants to be when he grows up. I haven't thought about that in a while. I just want to wake up tomorrow and know my family is safe.

Arnold begs Mr. Gearhart to let me tutor him in the hallway since I got an A on the test. Our teacher agrees, I think relieved to have Arnold out of class, unable to interrupt his teaching to take a class poll about the best Kentucky Derby winner.

We gather our things and sit down in the hallway next to the classroom door.

I flip open my textbook as we lean against the lockers. "You need math help?" I ask Arnold.

He chuckles and shakes his head. "Hah. No. I just thought we could use a break. Let's hang out."

Arnold pulls *The Daily Racing Form* from his back pocket, flipping through the pages and scanning the horses. I'm relieved for the quiet of the hallway and the chance to just sit with Arnold and be. He never asked me to explain what happened in the bathroom last week.

I open my math notebook and continue drawing a house plan I started yesterday. I need to add more rooms.

Alejandro's sister arrived at Prima Benita's yesterday.

Valeria and Alejandro spent the day before organizing her room and clearing two drawers in Valeria's dresser for Marisol. Sister Anne arranged to have Marisol take a bus from the Everglades Refugee Camp to the Catholic Welfare Bureau. From there, Prima Benita picked her up and brought her home. Prima Benita didn't make Alejandro go to school yesterday. She let him ride with her when she went to pick up Marisol.

Alejandro's little sister is a miniature version of him—dark eyes and hair with an uneasy smile. He talked up a storm yesterday, showing her every single corner of the small house. Marisol followed him around, not saying much and mostly looking tired.

But now I need to add more rooms to my house plans. I have a big room with a large window for Mami and Papi. Abuelo and Abuela's room looks out on a grove of mango trees I drew. Pepito has his own room shaped like a horseshoe. It wraps around my room.

But I decided to add another section of the house.

Rooms for Alejandro, Valeria, and Marisol. Even Prima Benita has her own room.

Everyone under one roof.

"So do they have horse races in Cuba?" Arnold asks, pulling me from concentrating on my plans.

I shrug. "No."

"Oh," Arnold says, disappointed. "So Cubans don't like horse races?"

I groan and take a deep breath. "I don't know. In Santa Clara, no horse races. Cuba? I don't know. Maybe."

Arnold nods, a smile returning to his face. "I get it. Just because you didn't have horse races in your part of Cuba doesn't mean there weren't any."

I think about Arnold's words and nod in agreement.

He points to my house plans and says, "I was going to ask if all Cubans had big houses like that, but I don't think that's right, either."

"No, not right," I tell him. "I am not a Cuban ambassador. I am Cumba."

Arnold nods, his eyes back to scanning the racing form. "Understood. But just for the record, everybody in the United States likes horse races."

"Not true."

"And everyone in the United States thinks that

hot dogs taste like tubes of cow manure and that hamburgers with ketchup, and definitely no mustard, are the best."

I narrow my eyes at Arnold, catching only a few of the words he said.

He clears his throat and gives me a thumbs-down. "Hot dogs bad." He flips his thumb up. "Hamburgers good."

"If you say so," I tell him, chuckling.

"Oh, I do say so." Arnold stands, hands on his hips and his chin jutting in the air. "I am your American ambassador."

I laugh again and shake my head.

Two girls walk by and snicker at us. "Oooh, look who got in trouble," they whisper to each other.

"We're not in trouble," Arnold calls down the hallway, sitting back down next to me. "We're just too smart for that class."

I clench my pencil until I think it might snap in two. I bang the back of my head on the locker.

"Whoa, Cumba, it's okay," Arnold tells me, looking startled. "Those girls were just talking nonsense."

I flip open my math textbook, my hands shaking. "We need to work. We should not lie. No trouble."

Arnold puts his hand on my arm. "Don't worry.

We won't get in trouble. It's not like we drew butts all over the lockers."

His reassurance doesn't make me feel any better. I want to tell Arnold that I can't mess up. If everyone thinks that everything I do is what all Cubans do, then I can't do anything wrong. It's all my responsibility to show them who Cubans are.

But I don't know enough English to tell him all that. So I simply say what Mami told me.

"I have to represent Cuba well."

CHAPTER 23

Arnold places another card down on the cafeteria table. "What's this one?" he asks me.

I know the person on the card está riendo, but I can't quite find the word in the filing cabinets in my brain. Sometimes I think it can hold only so much, and one day all the English I'm trying to shove in there will make me forget things.

I'm lucky I still know how to tie my shoes.

I squint at the card as if the answer is written in the stick figure's wide smile. Their body looks like it's tilted back a little, and their left hand is over their stomach. They're silly cards that Arnold drew to help me learn English verbs.

I finally pull out the right word from my brain. I slap my palm on the table, shaking the Jell-O on my lunch tray. "Laugh!" I tell Arnold.

He gives me a thumbs-up. He puts another card on the table. This one is easy, and I quickly shoot back, "Read."

Arnold quizzes me on the rest of the cards. I miss only three. I repeat over in my head *sing*, *smile*, and *jump*.

I nearly spit out my Jell-O when I see the card Arnold has drawn for "to pee."

"Cumba, this is a really important word. You gotta know this one, man," he assures me.

As best as I can, I tell Arnold that this has become an important verb in my house lately.

Five people in a house with one bathroom is proving to be a challenge. Last night, I took a shower at midnight.

I think Alejandro peed in the backyard yesterday when Valeria was taking too long in the bathroom.

Prima Benita says she gets letters from Cuban parents every week asking her to take in their children. So many parents are willing to send their kids all by themselves to a new country, just to escape Fidel, the brainwashing of the Young Rebels, and dangerous military service.

I think Prima Benita would take in the whole country if she could.

But there's no way her bathroom is big enough.

When Arnold and I finish the deck, he pulls out a small newspaper from underneath his cafeteria tray. "All right, Cumba. Let's pick 'em," he says.

He scrunches his nose as he scans *The Daily Racing Form*, listing all the horse races that will run. I like to translate the names of the horses, even though they usually don't make sense.

"One of these days, Cumba, we'll go to Gulfstream Race Track and bet on the winning horse. Make so much money you can buy Cuba."

I slap Arnold on the back and grin.

I would bet on a million horses.

After school, I head out the front doors, ready to walk toward Prima Benita's house. But I spot a red-and-white Chevrolet Bel Air taking up two spaces in front of Ponce de León Junior High School.

It's Prima Benita's car.

I walk up to the car and find Prima Benita sitting in the front seat. She has a worried look on her face. She leans over and opens the passenger door.

"Did you hear from my family? Did something happen to them?" I ask breathlessly as I slide into the front seat.

"No, Cumba. This isn't about your family," she says, patting my hand. "We need to go visit an office."

She wrings her hands on the steering wheel and

lowers her head. I hear her mutter, "There's just so many of you. I never imagined there'd be so many of you."

I clutch my schoolbooks to my chest. "Prima Benita, what's going on?"

"More children are arriving. I have three that will be here next week."

I wonder how eight people are going to function in Prima Benita's small house. I wonder if I'll ever be able to go to the bathroom inside again.

And then it hits me.

"I don't get to stay with you anymore, do I?" I say. I look out the window and watch the other kids at school walk down the sidewalk, laughing and smiling.

"No, Cumba. There's just no room. We're going to go to a foster care agency, and they'll place you with a family who can take care of you."

"Until my family gets here," I say, swallowing hard.

"Yes," Prima Benita says, gripping my hand. "Until your family gets here."

She drives through the streets of Miami, dodging cars and pedestrians. I begin to think maybe it wouldn't be so bad if she just drove straight off the Miami River bridge and into the water.

Just let the caja de muertos win.

Prima Benita explains that she's the only one of our family in the United States when I ask if there are any other cousins I can stay with. She says the Methodist Church is helping her place me, Alejandro, and Marisol with families now that her house is overcrowded. It doesn't make me feel much better knowing that Alejandro and Marisol have to leave, too.

We arrive at a plain office building. The flower bushes outside have been overtaken by kudzu vine. They'll probably be dead in a few months.

When we walk into the building, we're ushered to an office. The thought that I have to start all over again, in a new house, a new school, maybe even a new town, presses down on my shoulders. It makes me too tired to try to understand the conversation between Prima Benita and the bald man dressed in a suit that seems three sizes too large. He keeps stretching his arms out and pulling the sleeves of his suit up.

They talk for what feels like an eternity. I watch another child sitting in a glass-walled office. She looks younger than Pepito and has messy blond hair that's never met a comb. She's clutching a worn teddy bear, which is so raggedy it looks like it's been dipped in the toilet by a tormenting brother. I wonder if she gets to decide where she can live or if she has to let adults talk all around her, making decisions for her. I wonder if she has a caja de muertos tucked somewhere in her wrinkled pink dress.

"Does that sound good, Cumba?" the bald man asks, snapping me from my thoughts.

I look at Prima Benita. I understand what the man has asked me, but I have no idea what he's talking about.

"Key Largo, Cumba. How does Key Largo sound?" Prima Benita clarifies.

I shrug, knowing Abuela would give me a quick cocotazo for being impolite.

"Fine, I guess," I tell her.

I don't even know where that is.

The bald man hands me a piece of paper. "This is your family," he says.

The card says PHILLIP AND JEAN REYNOLDS, KEY LARGO, FLORIDA.

They aren't my family.

Ramón Fernandez is my father. He plays the clarinet better than anyone I know.

Margarita De Valle Fernandez is my mother. Her red fingernails always match her red lips, and she makes the best flan in all of Cuba.

Pepito Carlos Fernandez is my brother. He wants to be a cowboy when he grows up.

Josefina Fernandez is my grandmother. She sneaks me strawberry candies and galletas and always smells of lavender.

Juan Carlos Fernandez is my grandfather. He's strong enough to lift an entire pig or climb a coconut tree. When I was little, I thought he was a superhero.

That is my family. That is where I belong.

I don't know who Phillip and Jean Reynolds are, but they aren't my family.

And I'm certain I won't like them.

CHAPTER 24

The sidewalk is hot as the sun bears down on the benches where we sit in front of the Greyhound bus station downtown. Alejandro and Marisol are waiting for a bus to Naples so they can stay with a new family there. At least they have each other. I have no one.

I wait for my bus to the Keys, a scowl plastered to my lips and my hand shoved in my pocket, tightly wrapped around the caja de muertos. When Prima Benita told us where we were being sent, she showed us on an atlas. Naples is just across the state from Miami, while Key Largo is part of a series of islands that drip off the southern tip of Florida. They didn't seem too far apart on the map, but they might as well be on separate planets.

Before we left Prima Benita's house this morning for the bus station, I asked her to help me write a goodbye letter to Arnold. She promised to find his address and mail my note to him. I took a dollar I'd saved from my allowance and put it in the envelope. I told Arnold to bet on a horse we looked at in *The Daily Racing Form* yesterday.

His name was Soaring Freedom.

I watch as Valeria braids Marisol's hair in two long sections, jealous that Valeria gets to stay with Prima Benita and I don't. Alejandro sits down in a huff next to me on the bench.

"You know," he leans toward me and says, "if you have that look on your face when your new family sees you, they may think they're taking in a Cuban zombie."

I elbow him, looking away and trying not to smile. I'm fine staying camped in my grumpy mood.

Alejandro hits my arm with something. I turn and see him holding out my baseball glove.

"You never know," he tells me. "Maybe your new family plays baseball."

I kick my suitcase in front of me. "They aren't my new family. I already have a family."

Alejandro sets the glove on top of my suitcase. "I know. But take it anyway. Can't let you lose everything I've taught you. You have to represent Cuba well." He winks.

I close my eyes.

Represent Cuba well.

That's exactly what Mami said to me before I left.

I take a deep breath. Slouching on the bench, I take the caja de muertos out of my pocket and flip it between my fingers.

"Why do you always carry that thing with you?" Alejandro asks. "Is it special or something?"

"No, it's not special. It's just a reminder," I tell him, shoving the tile back into my pocket.

"A reminder of what?"

I sigh. "That I'll always be afraid. That I'll always be alone."

I rub my sweaty palms on my pants, not wanting to cry.

Alejandro grabs the baseball glove and holds it out to me again. "Well then, keep this so you can remember me."

I take my glove from him and run my fingers over the leather. There's a dirt mark at the top where I tried to field a ground ball and failed. The ball popped up and smacked me on the bottom of the chin. There's also a guava stain on the outside where Alejandro and I tried to play catch and eat Valeria's pastelitos at the same time. It was a messy failure.

I look at Alejandro. He brushes his hair aside, revealing an almost entirely faded scar.

"You know, I never had a little brother. But if I did . . ." Alejandro looks at me and winks. "He'd be a much better baseball player than you."

I sigh. "I don't have a big brother, but if I did . . . he would've warned me about oatmeal long before you did."

Alejandro laughs as I put the baseball glove in my suitcase.

A large silver bus pulls up, its brakes squeaking. The black-and-white sign at the top of the front window declares KEY LARGO.

My bus has arrived.

I swallow hard as Alejandro stands and grabs my suitcase. Valeria comes over to us and gives me a weak smile. I try not to look her or Alejandro in the eye.

Taking my suitcase from Alejandro, I step toward the bus.

"Cumba, wait," Alejandro says, grabbing my arm. He laces his fingers through my free hand as Valeria takes my suitcase, sets it on the sidewalk, and wraps her hand around mine. She and Alejandro grasp hands, and we stand in a small circle on the sidewalk.

I stare at the ground, shaking my head. The tears I had to hold back four months ago at the Havana airport when I said goodbye to my family, the tears held hostage by the soldiers watching us, come spilling from my eyes.

"Oh, Cumba," Valeria says, squeezing my hand and resting her head on my shoulder. "It'll be okay. You have to promise me that you'll have hope."

My chin quivers, tears still sliding down my cheeks.

Squeezing my hand even harder, she continues, "You have to hope for your family. You have to hope for your country. I know that effort might make your eyeballs pop out, but try."

Her hand trembles in mine as Alejandro lets out a loud chuckle to cover up a sob.

Valeria has too much faith in me. I didn't want to leave my family in Cuba. I don't want to leave this family I've made in Miami. I don't want to keep saying goodbye.

Alejandro lets go of our hands and grips my shoulders. "Hermanito, listen."

I wince at his calling me "little brother" so easily. Especially when it sounds so right.

He clears his throat and looks me in the eyes. I notice tears pooling in the corners of his.

"You're Cuban. You always will be," he says. "It's in your blood. It doesn't matter where we are. We'll always have that to hold us together."

Valeria nods enthusiastically and rubs my arm. "He's right, Cumba. We can live in the United States the rest of our lives. They can bury our bones here. But we'll always be Cuban."

Alejandro and Valeria wrap me in their arms as I cry. I don't want to let go of the soft fabric of Alejandro's shirt, the smoothness reminding me of Papi's suits. Valeria wears the same perfume as Mami. I breathe in the scent and let it fill my memories.

We stand in a huddle on the sidewalk as bus passengers disembark and the driver calls for new passengers. I hold Alejandro and Valeria even tighter, trying to squeeze the hope they so easily have into my body.

I want to believe that everything will be fine. That maybe we'll meet again when Valeria and her husband have five kids and Alejandro has won the World Series. We'll meet again when I've built skyscrapers in every city in the United States.

We'll meet again when Cuba is free.

CHAPTER 25

Dear Pepito,

I'm leaving. No, I'm not coming back to Cuba like you asked. I can't. I want to, but I can't. Prima Benita's house is too crowded. She's supposed to take in three siblings, two sisters and a brother, soon, so there wasn't any more room in her house for us.

I had to say goodbye to the only friends I've made since I came to the United States. Valeria, who has a laugh just like Mami's. Alejandro, who's not as tough as he seems. Arnold, who I'll probably read about in the newspaper someday in a horse-handicapping scheme. I'll miss the way he scrunched up his nose every time he'd look over <u>The Daily Racing Form</u>. He'll probably miss my math skills, which helped him figure out which horses had the best chances at winning.

And Prima Benita. She reminded me of Abuela. I'll

miss the shuffle of her slippers in the kitchen as she made our oatmeal.

But I won't miss the oatmeal.

Am I always going to be saying goodbye? Am I always going to think about people who are no longer here?

I'm sorry, Pepito, I don't mean to complain. I don't know what's going on with you. Are Mami and Papi back? Are you still staying with Abuelo and Abuela? Please let me know as soon as you can.

And make sure you write back to the address on this envelope. That's my new address in Key Largo.

Take care, Pepito. Be safe. I miss you.

Cumba

The Greyhound bus doesn't have air-conditioning. Most of the windows are open but are circulating only warm air. I'm riding down to Key Largo in an oven.

I watch clusters of houses give way to tall pines and palm trees. Eventually the land surrenders completely and the sea stretches out before us as the bus crawls along a long bridge. Is the bus driver taking me back to Cuba?

I lean forward in my seat on the bus, my back

sticky with sweat. I'm wearing the same suit I wore when I flew on a large metal beast away from Fidel. I grip the armrest in my seat as the bus heads south. Each mile takes me closer to Fidel. Closer to my family.

The long bridge carrying us over the blue water finally lands on an island. A large sign reads WELCOME TO KEY LARGO.

I guess I've arrived.

Key Largo has the same concrete buildings that Miami did, but most aren't taller than two stories. There are the same palm trees and pines but also a large number of mangroves bordering the shore.

The bus stops at the station in Key Largo. The other passengers grab their suitcases and file out of the bus. The men fan themselves with their hats as the women adjust their hairstyles, damp with perspiration. I wait for them to pass, fine with being the last to get off the bus.

Once the last passenger disembarks, I grab my suitcase and step off. I have no idea what Phillip and Jean Reynolds look like. Maybe they'll have a sign. Maybe they've seen a picture of me. Maybe they're secretly Mami and Papi, and they had to change their names to come to the United States.

See, Valeria, I want to say, *I can have hope, too.*

"Cumba?" a woman approaches me and says. "Are you Cumba?"

I look at her. She has blond hair the color of sand and a dress green like the palm trees perched behind her.

"Yes, I am Cumba," I tell her. I stick out my hand, recalling Mami's reminder to represent Cuba well.

The woman takes my hand and shakes it vigorously. "Wonderful! I'm Jean Reynolds."

And those are the last words I understand. She claps her hands together and begins a rapid-fire speech. I know it must be all good words because she's smiling and her eyes are gleaming.

A man in a light blue suit comes up beside her and puts his hand on her back.

"Jean, slow down, dear," he says.

Yes, Jean, please slow down, I think.

"Hi there, son," the man says, sticking out his hand. "Phillip Reynolds."

"Hello, Mr. Reynolds." I shake his hand. "I am Cumba. Nice to meet you."

Mr. Reynolds smiles. His straight posture and squared shoulders remind me of some of the soldiers in Cuba, except his easy smile isn't covered by a greasy black beard.

Phillip and Jean Reynolds guide me to their car.

"1958 Buick Roadmaster," I tell them. "Very nice."

Mr. Reynolds laughs. "Excellent!"

I slide into the back seat, the leather squeaking against my sweaty suit.

Mr. Reynolds backs up the car carefully, crawls to a stop at each stop sign, and accelerates slowly. He and Prima Benita must not have learned to drive from the same person.

We make small talk on our way, and I do my best to understand what they're saying. Mr. Reynolds does a good job of speaking clearly and slowly. I don't have too much trouble understanding what he's asking me.

"How was your bus ride?"

"Very hot."

"Do you like Florida?"

"It is very nice."

Mrs. Reynolds is a little harder to understand. I'm sitting right behind her, so I can't see her face. I didn't realize how much I rely on that when I'm trying to decipher what someone is saying. She's also speaking very quickly, but I get the impression it's just because she's excited.

"So what do you like to eat?" she asks.

This is definitely a question I can answer.

"I like chicken, black beans, rice. I like guava and cream cheese. I like pastelitos."

"Well, you might have to teach me how to make some of those," she responds.

I feel a tinge of guilt in my stomach. I don't want her to feel bad. She's taking a strange boy into her house, after all.

"I like hamburgers and french fries," I add.

"Oh, me too," she says, her blond hair blowing in the ocean breeze from the rolled-down window.

I bite my lip and think, wondering what else I can add. "But I don't like oatmeal."

Mr. Reynolds laughs and slaps the steering wheel. "Son, nobody likes oatmeal."

CHAPTER 26

The Reynoldses' house sits right on the beach, a two-story concrete structure daring the wind and waves to pummel it. Mrs. Reynolds takes me upstairs to my room, which is next door to the room of the Reynoldses' son, Nathaniel. Mrs. Reynolds tells me Nathaniel is five and a "whirling dervish." I don't know what that is.

After dinner, I sit at the dining room table and stare at the photos on the wall. Mr. Reynolds is in his military uniform. He looks dignified and proud. There's a photo of Mr. and Mrs. Reynolds on their wedding day, the same look of happiness that Mami and Papi have in theirs.

I reach into my pocket and pull out the caja de muertos. Eighteen dots. I can count eighteen people in my family that I miss. That are far away across the sea. Parents, grandparents, my brother, aunts, uncles, cousins. For my whole life, they made me who I was. But now that I'm alone, who am I?

"Do you like to play dominoes?" Mr. Reynolds asks, carrying a cup of coffee into the dining room.

"Yes, I do like it," I tell him. "Do you like to play dominoes?"

Mr. Reynolds goes over to the dark brown hutch lining the dining room wall and opens the bottom drawer. He reaches in and pulls out a rectangular wooden box. Setting it on the table, he says, "I don't play dominoes very much, but I love chess. Do you like chess?"

I scrunch my eyebrows and think about the word he used. I don't know it. "Chess?"

Mr. Reynolds opens the box and takes out a board covered in squares and small black and white pieces. "Oh," I exclaim. "Ajedrez."

Mr. Reynolds takes a sip of his coffee and arranges the pieces on the board. He points to each piece and says its name. I repeat the names over in my head to try to remember them.

Rook. Rook. Rook.

Knight. Knight. Knight.

Pawn. Pawn. Pawn.

Bishop. Bishop. Bishop.

Queen. Queen. Queen.

King. King. King.

Mr. Reynolds shows me how each piece is allowed to move on the board. It's easy to understand him because all the words he uses are numbers and directions. One space forward. One space left, two spaces forward. One space diagonal.

We play a slow game as I look to Mr. Reynolds for assurance each time I move a piece. He's patient with me and smiles each time I place my finger on a chess piece.

We hear laughter come from the bathroom as Mrs. Reynolds helps Nathaniel take a bath.

This is a happy house. A loving family.

But it's still not my house. Or my family.

I don't have to start school until Tuesday, so I make a new schedule at the Reynoldses' house. Nathaniel and I play each morning on the beach behind the house, trying to find as many different seashells as we can. Nathaniel wants to take them into the house to give to his mom, but I tell him it's bad luck. In the afternoon, Mrs. Reynolds has me teach her how to make Cuban food. I don't have the heart to tell her that I didn't really pay attention when Mami and Abuela concocted their wonders in the kitchen; I was just the ever-ready taste tester. Mrs. Reynolds blames her lack of success making croquetas, pastelitos, and picadillo on her cooking ability rather than my horribly made-up instructions. But I like how she asks me questions.

"Does your mami add one egg or two? Did your grandma cook the chicken with onions or green peppers?"

She doesn't make me think I'm telling her how an entire island makes flan or arroz con pollo. Just how the Fernandez family does it. I'm not a Cuban ambassador to her. I'm Cumba, a boy from Cuba.

Each evening, Mr. Reynolds and I escape to his office and play chess. I've beaten him only once. I can't decide if he let me win.

It's a nice routine that makes me forget the oncoming storm that might blow me completely off the island.

School.

CHAPTER 27

Dear Pepito,

I'm starting school today. Again. At least this time I understand a little more English. I understand that teachers want you to be quiet. I understand that you have to learn to swim down the hallway with the sea of noise.

I wonder if this school will be different. Will my history teacher scratch his fat gut while the class reads over and over like trained dogs? Will I find a horse-racing enthusiast with freckles to make lunchtime more bearable?

I guess we'll see.

I drew you a picture of the new house where I'm living. It's two stories, and Nathaniel, the Reynoldses' son, likes to jump up and down the stairs. My room is the biggest I've ever had. Big enough for you and me. For Mami and Papi, too. It's right above the kitchen, and I can smell the coffee that Mrs. Reynolds makes when I wake up in the morning. Abuelo would say it isn't strong enough. The house sits right on the beach, and I can hear the ocean through my window. Maybe if I shout loud enough over the waves, you can hear me.

There's a lot more I want to ask you. But I know you'll tell me if something new happens.

Your brother,
Cumba

The sound of actual ocean waves mixes in with the waves of noise coming from Coral Shores Junior High School. Mr. Reynolds stands next to me, his hat in his hands.

"Are you ready, Cumba?" he asks, rubbing his thumb on the brim of his hat, just like Papi always does.

Claro que no, I want to say, but I simply mumble, "Yes, sir."

We walk into the building, and Mr. Reynolds guides me to the school office. He says something to the woman perched behind a desk, and she guides us into a small office with the word COUNSELOR written on the front.

As we sit down, a man walks in wearing a short-sleeved white button-down shirt and black pants. He's the tallest man I've ever seen. I think he must've ducked to make it through the doorway. Sitting down in his chair, he still towers over Mr. Reynolds and especially over me.

"Good morning, Cumba. I'm Mr. Ferguson," he says with a smile that pushes his thick, black-rimmed glasses up his nose, reminding me of Padre Tomás. "Welcome to Coral Shores."

"Thank you, sir," I tell him. I'm relieved that he speaks slowly and clearly. He looks me in the face when he talks.

"Let's get you some classes," Mr. Ferguson says, pulling out a file from a drawer in his desk. "Obviously, you will take math, science, history, and English. But you get to pick three other classes that you'd like to take."

I think about what he's told me and run his words over again in my head. "I pick my classes?" I ask him for confirmation.

"Yes. This is a list of electives," he says, handing me a piece of paper.

I don't understand the last word he says, but I take the paper and look it over. Some of the words on the paper I understand.

"I take physical education. Art."

Mr. Ferguson nods and scribbles on the paper on his desk. I know I need one more class, but I don't know any of the other words on the paper. I try my luck as the caja de muertos in my pocket taunts me.

One of the classes listed says "shop." That's what Mami does all the time. I don't think I want to take a shopping class.

The class above that says "home economics." I know the word *home*, but I don't know the second word. Maybe we learn how to make homes. I love building things. I want to be an architect when I'm older. So that class sounds good to me.

I clear my throat. "Home economics, please," I tell Mr. Ferguson.

I watch a smile creep at the corner of his lips. "Are you sure?"

I scrunch my eyebrows. Why wouldn't I be sure? "Yes, sir. I am sure."

"All right, son, if that's what you want. I think a lot of the other classes are full anyway."

Mr. Ferguson writes down my schedule and hands it to me. I look it over. My first class is history. Again.

"Would you like me to walk with you to your first class?" Mr. Ferguson asks, standing. He towers above me. I wonder how many inches he has until he brushes the ceiling with his blond hair. Walking down the hall with him would definitely make me stand out to every single student at Coral Shores Junior High School. That's not something I want.

"No thank you, sir. I find my class," I tell him.

We shake hands, I say goodbye to Mr. Reynolds, and I head out into the hallway, bracing myself against the hurricane of noise.

Maybe it's the salty sea air. Maybe it's the fact that you can look out the window and watch the waves crashing on the beach. Maybe it's the lychee nut and coconut trees around the school grounds begging you to pick up their fallen fruit. But this school is different.

In history class, I stared at our textbook, the words once again jumbling in my head. I waited for the students to read, one by one, a march of words I wouldn't understand. Instead, the teacher showed us lots of pictures. She pointed at various objects and people in the pictures and named them. It made it a lot easier for me to understand.

When it was time to read in our textbooks on our own, she walked over to me and handed me a black pen and a red pen. Pointing to the black pen, she said, "This is for important words you know." She tapped her finger to her head and then gave me a thumbs-up. Then she pointed to the red pen and explained, "This is for the important words you don't know." She once again pointed to her temple but then gave me a thumbs-down. I was pretty sure I understood what she said, but her gestures just confirmed my thoughts.

"I write in the textbook?" I asked, unsure if she was really telling me to write all over school property.

Crouching down next to me, she said, "Don't worry. These books are older than I am," and gave me a broad smile.

The same thing continued in English and science class. The teachers used a lot of pictures and had me list words I knew and didn't know. It was like they could sense my difficulties before I even had them.

Math class was great. We did calculation races, and I actually got first place at one point. Several students gave me a thumbs-up.

And then I walked into home economics. I was eager to further my knowledge of architecture. I pictured myself working in an office one day, building models and plans of all the buildings I would design.

When I walked into the classroom, I saw it had sinks and ovens. Instead of desks, there were long tables.

I don't think home economics means what I thought it meant.

"Ay Dios mío, it's Fidel!" shouts a voice from the corner of the classroom.

I spin on my heels. I know that voice.

A dark-haired boy jumps up from his stool and races over to me.

It's Serapio.

He wraps me in his arms, and we give each other a tight hug. I hear students giggle around us, but I don't care.

When we finally pull away, we shoot questions at each other in rapid-fire Spanish.

"What are you doing here?" I ask him.

"You think I got all those shots in my butt for nothing? I was coming here just like you, but my abuela told me not to tell."

"Mine too. Who are you staying with?"

Serapio chuckles. "Some American lady that I think was born before Cuba shot up out of the ocean. But she's nice enough. Has a small fishing boat that she lets me take out."

We're flailing our arms around as we speak because, well, that's just how we talk. The giggling around us increases as the teacher approaches, her heels clicking on the linoleum floor.

"Gentlemen, please sit down," she says with pursed, wrinkled lips.

Serapio pulls me to the stool next to his. I look around and notice we're the only two boys in the class.

"Oye, Cumbito, I'm glad you're here and all. You know, bienvenidos a los estados unidos and all that . . . but you're ruining my chances," Serapio says with a smirk.

"Your chances?"

"Yeah, until you got here, I was the only boy in this class. The cute foreign boy who just needs to be taken care of." Serapio gives me a puppy dog look.

I groan. "If you say so, chico."

The teacher snaps her fingers at the front of the classroom. "Girls, today we are going to make apple turnovers."

The questions tumbling in my head raise my eyebrows. First, I'm not a girl. Second, how do you get an apple to turn over?

This isn't going to end well.

CHAPTER 28

Dear Pepito,

You won't believe who's at my school. Never in a million years.

Serapio!

It's so much better having someone I know at school. I don't feel so alone. And it's nice to have someone to speak Spanish with and to help me out at school. Although I have a sneaking suspicion Serapio doesn't tell me the right English words sometimes. I'm pretty sure I cursed at a girl in my home economics class today.

Oh, and home economics isn't what you think it is.

Your brother,
Cumba

Mr. Reynolds scratches his eyebrow as he contemplates his next move. His hand rests on the rook, and I can't keep a smirk from growing on my face. I've learned a lot about chess in the past two weeks. He catches my smile and removes his hand from the rook. My shoulders sag.

I look at the pictures hanging on the wall of his office while he thinks about how to defeat me. There's a picture of him in a military uniform.

"You are in the army?" I ask him.

Mr. Reynolds moves a pawn and says, "No, I was in the navy. In World War II."

I think about his words. "What do you do in the navy?"

"I flew airplanes," he responds, waving his hand for me to take my turn.

I examine the board. He has me cornered. I chew on my lip. "You fly P-51 Mustang?"

Mr. Reynolds slaps his leg. "Hah! I wish. That's an incredible airplane, isn't it? But all show. I flew an F4F Wildcat. Used to fly it right off a ship. Now that's something."

Mr. Reynolds and I have played chess every night after dinner for the last two weeks. We chat during our games, and I found out that Mr. Reynolds worked in Japan after the war. He pointed out on a map where Japan is. He showed me his diploma from Yale University and told me it was the best school in the country to go to. When he showed me where in the United States Yale University is, I asked him if it was cold where it was. He said yes.

I decided I didn't want to go there.

"My dad is in the army before. But he does not fly planes. He is a lawyer now."

Mr. Reynolds looks at me. I don't know what he knows about my family. How much the people who sent me here told him, if they knew anything at all.

"Well, your dad has a very good job. An important job."

I puff up my chest and smile.

"I want to be an architect. I love math."

The smile on Mr. Reynolds's face grows to the biggest I've ever seen. He laughs and says, "Don't you know what I do, Cumba?"

"No, sir," I reply.

With one sweep of his arm, Mr. Reynolds slides all our chess pieces back into the box. He gets up, goes to his desk, and pulls out a roll of large papers. Slipping off the rubber band around them, he lays them out on the table between us. Lines, angles, and numbers stare up at me.

"I'm an architect. These are my blueprints." Mr. Reynolds puts his hands on his hips.

I point to the papers. "Blueprints?" I test out the word in my mouth.

"Yes. This is for a new government building here in Islamorada that was destroyed in Hurricane Donna."

We spend the next hour going over the blueprints as Mr. Reynolds explains what the symbols and numbers on the paper mean. He gives me a blank piece of paper, and we start to draw out our own blueprint of my house in Santa Clara. I close my eyes and picture my home. How you could walk from the backyard, through the kitchen, turn left down the hall, and then turn left again into my room. He asks me to picture in my head how many steps it would take to do that, and from that information, we figure out how big to make my house on the blueprints. Whenever I don't understand something Mr. Reynolds says, he always rephrases it or uses hand motions to explain. He even draws on the paper at one point when I don't understand the word *roof*.

"And just what are you gentlemen doing?" Mrs. Reynolds asks, pulling us from our hunched positions over the paper. "It's after midnight!"

I look at the clock in Mr. Reynolds's office. We've been drawing our blueprints for three hours.

Mr. Reynolds has me sign the bottom of our blueprints. "All architects put their name on their work," he explains. He rolls up the paper just like his blueprints and puts a rubber band around it.

I thank him and shuffle up the stairs to my room. Unrolling the paper, I spread out the blueprints on my lap as I sit on my bed. I trace my finger from Mami's dental office in the front, through our living room, into the kitchen, and out into the backyard. I picture the coconut tree in the back, Abuelo climbing to the top and scaring Abuela. I draw a square around Mami and Papi's room and hear the sound of Papi snoring loudly. I place my hand over the front of the house and see the poinciana and mango trees, complete with the tocororo pecking at a fallen fruit.

Rolling the blueprints back up, I place them carefully on the top of my dresser and notice the caja de muertos lying next to them.

I realize I forgot to put it in my pocket today.

CHAPTER 29

Dear Cumba,

Mami and Papi are home. I want to fill up this entire page with that sentence. Mami and Papi are home.

They won't tell me what happened. I tried to listen in when Papi and Abuelo were talking, but Abuela made me go to my bedroom. Papi has a black eye, and his lip looks cut. Abuela has to change bandages on his wrists. Mami has a bruised cheek, and I notice she limps on her left leg when she thinks I'm not looking. She's still as pretty as ever, of course, but her eyes look sad. Abuela won't tell me why her eyes look sad.

There's a lot more whispering in the house. Every night, I go to bed to the sound of whispering. They won't tell me what they're talking about. Nobody tells me anything.

So tell me about your new home, tell me something, tell me anything.

Your brother,
Pepito

I'm kneeling on the floor, sobbing, the letter clutched in my hand, when Mrs. Reynolds comes into my room.

"Cumba! Are you okay?" she asks, rushing over to me.

I wipe the tears from my cheeks and sit on my bed. "Yes, ma'am," I tell her. "I am fine, thank you."

"What's wrong?" Mrs. Reynolds puts her hand on my back. I want to hug her, to sob with happiness into her shoulder, but I don't want her to think I'm crazy.

It's harder to form the words in my head when I'm crying. Every time I get a sentence in order, it's washed away by the flood of tears. I finally manage to spit out, "My parents in jail. Now they are home."

Mrs. Reynolds sighs. "Oh, Cumba. That's good."

She pats my leg as we listen to the ocean waves crash outside through the open window.

"I know it's difficult being away from them. I know it's difficult being alone. But they will be here soon. You will all be together."

I shove my hand into my pocket and wrap it around the caja de muertos.

Everyone wants me to have hope. Everyone wants me to think that things will get better. But my parents have been beaten. While they may finally be home, I don't want to think about what they went through before they got there.

"Yes, ma'am," I mumble.

It's hard to argue with hopeful people. Especially when the doubt in your head mixes up your English words.

"Oye, Cumbito," Serapio says when I get to school. "What're the Cuban ambassadors doing today?"

I chuckle and shake my head. Serapio and I are the only two Cubans at Coral Shores Junior High, so once again, we're the representatives for an entire country.

Serapio's hips start to move side to side as his feet shuffle. I groan as he salsas in front of his locker, humming a tune. Two girls point and laugh behind him, and he twirls and faces them.

"That's how Cubans do," he proclaims, raising his arms.

The girls' laughter grows louder, and they sprint away.

I sigh. "Por Dios, I'm not hanging out with you anymore."

I shove my hands into my pockets. I have Pepito's letter tucked in one pocket around the caja de muertos. Maybe if I'm lucky, the worn paper I've read over and over will dissolve the tile and make it disappear. But a different paper in my other pocket is my mission today.

"I have to go see Miss Cochran," I tell Serapio.

"But why?" Serapio groans. "I can teach you all the English you need to know, chico. Everything you need for the ladies."

I roll my eyes and give Serapio a shove on the shoulder as I head to Miss Cochran's classroom. Knocking on the doorframe, I clear my throat and say, "Excuse me, Miss Cochran?" Her last name still twists on my tongue, and I know I always say it wrong. Still, she greets me with a wide smile.

"Hi, Cumba," she says, sitting at her desk and twirling a pencil around her long fingers. "How are you? It's a bit hot today, isn't it?"

"I am okay, thank you. Yes, it's very hot today." I like that Miss Cochran always asks me questions she knows I can answer, her green eyes glinting every time I speak English. I pull the folded paper out of my pocket and hand it to her. The words written on it are a mystery, one I want to solve.

"You please help me read this?" I ask her.

Miss Cochran scans the page, and a tight line forms at her lips. She sighs deeply as her eyes narrow at the page, confirming my suspicions.

This paper doesn't say anything good.

I spied an article in the newspaper as I was eating breakfast with the Reynoldses this morning. The words *Cuba* and *Cubans* were written a lot, which originally drew my attention. But then I spotted words like *problem* and *wrong*, and I needed to know what the article said.

Miss Cochran looks up from the paper at me. "You want to know what this says? Really?"

"Yes, please," I answer.

She motions me to a desk and slides another next to it, sitting down. "This is just one person's opinion. Understand?"

I nod. I still want to know what all the words mean.

For the next half hour, Miss Cochran lets me skip history class and spends her planning period flipping through a large Spanish-English dictionary to translate an article from the *Miami Herald*. We decipher sentences like *There are too many Cubans coming to the United States . . . It's wrong for the government to let them stay. They bring their problems, and we have to solve them . . . They should stay in their own country.*

I grip the corners of the desk as I stare at the translation I've written down. The caja de muertos is laughing at me through Pepito's letter.

What if the government changes its mind and Mami, Papi, my abuelos, and Pepito are stuck in Cuba? What if they decide to kick me out and send me back?

What if . . . ?

What if . . . ?

Miss Cochran grabs my hand and squeezes. "Cumba, listen," she says. "You belong here."

I take a deep breath. Miss Cochran takes the newspaper article off the desk and crumples it into a wadded ball, her knuckles turning white with the force of her grip. She stretches her arm back and throws the paper, sailing it through the air and into the trash can across the classroom.

She looks at me again. "You belong here."

CHAPTER 30

The blue sea stretches out before Serapio and me, laced with white-tipped waves. The boat bounces up and down as it crests each wave, and I'm not sure the crumbling boat with its wind-up toy motor is going to survive.

Serapio and I decided to take the boat out after school. Mrs. Dickinson, the woman Serapio lives with, promised to cook up any fish we caught. I don't think she understands what horrible fishermen we are. Serapio and I are from Santa Clara, in the middle of the mountains. Most Americans probably think that Cuba is such a small island that we all have houses right on the beach.

But Serapio and I are still trying. Unfortunately, Serapio's method is to try to chase the fish in our little boat. Each time he sees a school of fish jump in the water, he revs the boat engine and takes off after them. Of course, by the time we get to where we saw them jump, they're long gone.

"Oye, Serapito, this isn't working. We need to find a good spot and just stay there. The fish will come to us."

Serapio smirks. "A good fisherman waits for no fish."

"We're not good fishermen," I say, tossing a worm at him.

He brushes it off. "Vale. You want to wait for the little fishies, we'll wait for the little fishies."

Serapio pulls the boat near an outcropping of mangrove trees, their long roots perched in the water. We each stab a worm onto our hooks and lower them into the water. The boat rocks gently back and forth as the sun warms our backs.

These fish better hurry up, or I might fall asleep.

I peer into the water, looking to see if fish are circling the sandy bottom. Serapio nudges my arm and points to the horizon.

"You think we should just keep going? You think this little boat could make it?"

I shake my head. "This boat will be lucky to make it back to Mrs. Dickinson's."

I glance at Serapio. He looks at the horizon line, the blue water melting into the equally blue sky. He squints, as if he's trying to spot his abuela ninety miles away.

"You'd really go back?" I ask him.

He runs his thumb over the fishing line and picks at it with his fingernail. "I don't have anyone here. And I'm not waiting for anyone. My abuela isn't going to come over. She told me so. Why not go back? Fidel won't be there forever."

I think of Valeria waiting for Fernando. I think of Alejandro reunited with Marisol. I close my eyes and picture the day when I'll get to see Mami, Papi, and Pepito again. Maybe Abuelo and Abuela will even be with them.

But that day may never come.

Serapio reels in his fishing line, the worm stolen by a sneaky fish. "With our luck, Fidel made a deal with some Santero priest and will live forever."

I shake my head and chuckle. "Zombie Fidel. Yep, that sounds exactly like our luck."

I feel a tug on my line, like someone plucking a guitar string. "Oye, Serapito, I think I got one."

Serapio rocks the boat, moving to stand over me. He grabs our net, ready to scoop up the fish. "Reel it in! Reel it in!"

The tugs on my line grow stronger, and I spin the handle of my fishing rod as quickly as I can. I yank my rod back, and the fish on my line comes flying above the surface of the water.

Except it's not a whole fish, just a head. Its mouth is hooked on my line, but its body ends just after the gills, bright red blood dripping into the water.

Serapio pats me on the shoulder. "Looks like you made it easier for a barracuda to catch his dinner."

I grab the fishing line and pull the fish head off the hook, droplets of blood sprinkling my pants.

"You think Mrs. Dickinson knows how to make some kind of fish head soup?" I ask Serapio.

"Ay Dios mío, I'd never be *that* hungry."

"Yeah, me neither." I stand and take the fish head, launching it high into the air and back into the water, using my best form just like Alejandro taught me.

Serapio laughs and shouts, "Oye, a gift for you, Fidel! Just what you deserve!"

I laugh. We sit down in the boat. I try to wipe the fish blood off my pants but succeed in only smearing it into streaks.

I watch Serapio impale another worm on his hook, his teeth biting his lip in concentration.

"You know, you don't have to go back if you don't want to. You could live with my family when . . . *if* they come," I tell Serapio.

A smile creeps across the corner of Serapio's lips. "You really think your family's coming?"

I want to shout yes. I want to scream at the horizon. I want to jump up and down in the boat, waving my arms to let my family know where to come.

But the caja de muertos is heavy in my pocket, and it won't let me stand up.

"Ay Dios mío, I see a dolphin!" Serapio shouts, pointing down the mangrove bank.

He reels in his fishing line, and I do the same. I rev the boat engine and it sputters to life, pushing us down the shore.

"De veras, Serapito, I don't see any dolphins. And even if we find one, I don't think you're going to catch it with your fishing line."

Serapio bites his lip, thinking. "Bueno, maybe I'll just jump in the water and tackle it." He makes a muscle with his bicep. "Soy tan fuerte, ¿ya tú sabes?"

He may be strong, but I have a slight suspicion his dolphin-wrestling skills are as good as his fishing skills.

"It's over there now! Don't you see it?" Serapio speeds the sputtering boat up, chanting, "Ven aquí, delfín. ¡Ven aquí!"

The boat speeds around the corner of the cay, and Serapio cuts the engine when we see what's before us.

We're not the only boat here.

Four boats much larger than ours are pulled up between the mangroves and sea grape bushes. I count about ten men loading wooden crates onto the boats.

I look closely and spot one of the men holding a pistol while he gnaws on a cigar. Men with guns chomping on cigars is an all-too-familiar scene for me.

"Serapito, we need to go," I say, my voice shaking.

Instead of acknowledging my request, Serapio lets the current push us closer to the men and their boats.

"I just want to see what they're doing," he says.

One of the men looks up and notices us. He waves his pistol in our direction and shouts, "¡Véte de aquí, chicos! ¡Véte!"

The man is telling us to go away.

I stand up in the boat and raise my hands. "Lo siento, señor. Estábamos pescando. Buscando delfines."

I hope my innocent explanation that we were just fishing and looking for dolphins won't make them angry. Or point their guns in a direction I'd rather they didn't.

The men stop loading their boats and look at us. One of them smiles and slaps another on the arm. "¿Cubanos?"

"¡Claro!" Serapio shouts.

The men laugh and continue their work. The man who originally told us to go away slides his pistol into the waistband of his pants and motions us to come closer.

Serapio eases the boat forward.

"Are you sure?" I whisper to him.

He shrugs. "Sure, why not?"

I can think of a million reasons why not, but Serapio docks our boat on the shore anyway.

The man holds his hand out to me and says, "Come see what we have for Fidel."

I grab his rough, calloused hand, and he helps me out of the boat. Serapio jumps out and walks over to the stack of crates on the shore.

"Serapito, cuidado," I whisper to him, asking him to be careful. "They said this stuff is for Fidel. They might be working for him."

I hear a deep laugh behind me, and the man slaps me on the back, making me choke on my own spit.

"¿Trabajando por Fidel? Este mocoso . . ." He proceeds to unleash a string of words describing Fidel that wouldn't have just earned me a cocotazo from Abuela. She would've strung me up by my toes from the nearest mango tree.

The man opens a crate and shows us the contents hidden inside.

Serapio whistles. My eyes grow bigger than coconuts.

Inside the crate are rifles, revolvers, grenades, and more bullets than I've ever seen.

"¿Quieres probarlo?" the man asks us, jutting his chin toward a crate.

Serapio laughs and starts to reach for a grenade.

"If you lay one hand on that, I'm going to feed you to the sharks," I hiss at him.

The man laughs and launches brown cigar spit from his mouth. "Oye, tenemos un guerrero aquí, ¿no?"

"No, I'm not a fighter. My family sent me here by myself."

The man gnaws on his cigar and crosses his arms. "No te preocupes, guerrero. Don't worry. We'll get rid of Fidel. You'll be able to go back to your family soon."

I pull Serapio toward our boat, slapping his hand from keeping a grenade as a souvenir. We thank the men and tell them buena suerte, wishing them luck.

I really do wish them luck. I hope they storm the island and clear it of every single soldier that ever made me feel afraid. That made me look down every alley walking home from school. That made Pepito cry into my shoulder every night before going to sleep.

But if the good guys are shooting at the bad guys, how can I guarantee that my family won't get caught in the cross fire?

CHAPTER 31

Dear Cumba,

Why haven't you written? It's been two weeks, and Mami is worried that something has happened to you. Abuelo usually brings your letters straight to the house when they come to the post office. Each time he walks into the kitchen, Mami gets excited. But then he shows us his empty hands. Are you okay? Did something happen to you? You need to write. It's not good for Mami to worry.

   She has enough to worry about.

Your brother,
Pepito

I race to my bedroom and grab a piece of paper. I clench my pencil so hard it almost breaks in two. I search my brain for the right words to say.

How do I tell Pepito what really happened? That I wasn't sick or in danger.

Every day after school, Serapio and I go out on the boat and fish. Every evening after dinner, Mr. Reynolds and I sit in his office, drawing plans for buildings and houses.

I forgot to write.

I forgot my family.

I press my pencil to the paper, and the tip snaps against the page. I brush the broken lead away, leaving black streaks.

Closing my eyes, I picture Pepito. I'm sure he's grown since I last saw him six months ago at the airport. Does he still dress up in his cowboy costume? Does it even fit him anymore?

I can't tell him I just forgot to write. The look of disappointment on Mami's face, her lips pursed and eyes drooped, is not something I want to cause. I don't want them to think I replaced them with a new family. Mr. Reynolds isn't my dad. Mrs. Reynolds isn't my mom. Little Nathaniel isn't my brother, even though he makes me laugh just as much as Pepito.

But how is my heart supposed to survive, to pump and keep me going, if half of it is still across the ocean?

I remember sitting in the living room of my home in Santa Clara the night of my going-away party. I told Manuelito that sometimes you have to forget in order to survive being in a new place.

I didn't realize that would hurt so much.

Dear Pepito,

Wow, life in the United States sure is busy. People are always in a hurry to get everywhere. It's very easy to get caught up in that wave.

School keeps me busy with lots of homework. They talk at us and give us work eight hours each day and then want us to do even more work when we get home. I don't mind the math homework because I like it, and Mr. Reynolds helps me if I get stuck. But the English homework, I don't like. I'd rather talk to Mr. and Mrs. Reynolds to practice my English.

Serapio is just as crazy in the United States as he was in Cuba. He's convinced he's going to marry some blond American girl and take her back to Cuba with him when Fidel is gone. Can you imagine that? He's also certain he's the best fisherman in the Florida Keys, but, honestly, if I had to rely on him for my dinner, I would've died a month ago.

I'm okay. I'm doing well. Please tell Mami, Papi, and the abuelos not to worry about me. I just want to see you all here, too.

Your brother,
Cumba

⸻

I watch a small crab crawl out of its hole, snap its claws at me, and then retreat back into the sand. I brush the page of my notebook clean and stare at the blank lines again. Serapio and I decided to sit out on the shore in front of Mrs. Dickinson's house to work on a school project we were given by our history teacher.

As if the warm sea air might blow all the right answers directly into our brains.

Serapio groans next to me. "Oye, Cumbito. This Cuban ambassador basura is too much. My brain isn't working."

I flick a mosquito off my knee. "It may be garbage, but your brain usually isn't working regardless. Just write something down."

Last week our history teacher told us she wanted Serapio and me to give a special report on Cuba to the class. Never mind that neither of us speaks enough English to tell the class everything our teacher wants us to. Never mind that we never paid much attention to Padre Tomás during his Cuban history lectures.

Never mind that I'd rather wrestle a rabid squid than stand up and talk in front of the class.

"Fine," Serapio says, narrowing his eyes at his notebook. "What should we tell the Americanos about Cuba?"

My stomach grumbles, giving me an idea. "How about the food? I know that's not history, but it's Cuba. At this point, I don't care."

"I like it. I want to tell them all about picadillo and how the sweet raisins and sour olives make the perfect combination," Serapio says, practically drooling on his paper.

"My mami doesn't put raisins in picadillo," I counter. "How about eating empanadas for Nochebuena? We'd always have the leftovers on Christmas morning."

Serapio bites his lip. "Abuela and I always ate croquetas for Nochebuena."

I toss my notebook next to me and lie back on the sand. "Serapito, this isn't going to work. You know Mrs. Barnes wants us to agree and say, 'All Cubans do this; all Cubans are like this.'"

Serapio kicks the sand. "I don't remember signing up to be an ambassador."

"Me neither. But here we are. Let's just make something up and write it down."

Serapio and I hastily scrawl a paragraph about Christmas Eve in Cuba. We all eat lechón, empanadas, and flan. We sing songs and dance in the backyard. Sometimes we bang large metal spoons on pots and pans to make more noise, scaring the chickens that every single person in Cuba owns.

It's mostly true.

For any word we don't know in English, we circle what we've written in Spanish instead so Serapio can ask Mrs. Dickinson for help. He says she gives him a Hershey's kiss candy for each new English word he learns. Sometimes he asks her words he already knows just for more chocolate.

Serapio stands and brushes the sand off his pants. "We deserve a reward."

"We wrote five sentences."

Pulling me up from the beach, Serapio shakes his head. "Doesn't matter. The fish are waiting."

We abandon our notebooks on the sand and head toward the small dock in front of Mrs. Dickinson's house. Climbing into the boat, we sputter out into the waves.

This is always the best part of my day. When Serapio and I take the boat out, the sea air tangles my hair. Splashes of water dry on my skin, leaving behind sparkling specks of salt. The noise of school floats away on the waves. And if I squint just hard enough at the horizon, I can almost see home.

Serapio idles the engine down and brings the boat to a stop next to some mangroves along the shore. We pull our fishing rods from the bottom of the boat.

"Oye, Cumbito. Guess what we haven't done in a while. AFDF," Serapio says, dropping his fishing line into the water.

I smile. "Por Dios, I haven't thought about that in forever."

"So, before Fidel, we were boys from the mountains and terrible fishermen. After Fidel—"

"We're still terrible fishermen," I interrupt.

Serapio chuckles in agreement, tossing his fishing rod back into the boat. "Let's find a better spot."

"I don't think the spot matters," I say as the boat speeds south along the mangroves. I start to recognize where Serapio is heading.

My hands grip the sides of the boat. "Not this way, Serapito. I don't want to run into those guys again. It's too dangerous."

Seeing crates of weapons meant for my home made me nervous all over again for Mami, Papi, Pepito, and my abuelos.

Serapio doesn't slow the boat down. "They're not dangerous. They're trying to help. One of them is even from Santa Clara, like us."

I stare at Serapio. "How do you know that?"

Serapio purses his lips and juts his chin toward the shore. "I've been going to talk to them. To see if I can help."

My mouth drops open. I have a sinking suspicion that for the past three weeks the times my friend groaned about not being able to hang out after school because Mrs. Dickinson had a mountain of chores for him to do have been a lie.

"Stop the boat, Serapio," I say.

"No." The engine revs, and the small boat speeds faster along the shoreline, bouncing on the waves.

"Stop the boat!"

I lunge at Serapio's hand on the tiller, and the boat swerves, throwing us to the side. Finally letting go, Serapio stands as the boat jerks to a stop, swaying in the waves.

"What's your problem?" he shouts.

I climb to my feet, the boat rocking. "It's dangerous! What are you trying to do?"

Serapio's fists clench at his sides. "He took everything from me!" he screams, his face red, a bulging vein snaking up his neck. "You don't think I'm going to fight him for the rest of my life?"

I step back in the unsteady boat, the waves lapping against the metal sides.

I put my hands up in surrender. "I know, Serapito. But you can't—"

"Yes, I can!" Serapio shouts. His hands collide with my chest, and I tumble backward. My foot catches on the fishing rods lying on the bottom of the boat, and I lose my balance, falling over the edge and into the water.

The salt water stings my eyes and burns my throat as I suck it down. Flailing my arms, I push to the surface as the waves knock against me until I feel a strong grip on my hand. I look up and see Serapio, his eyes wide, straining to pull me back into the boat.

Throwing my leg over the side, I yank myself up as Serapio hauls me in under my arms. I slump into the bottom of the boat and my throat burns as I try to catch my breath. Serapio sits down across from me with a sigh and wipes his wet hands on his pants. I shake my head, spraying the boat with water.

I look at my friend, his head lowered, his fingers

knotted in his hair. His chest heaves. I'm certain he's crying. The boat rocks side to side, and I think of all the people we left across the waves.

I hear Serapio suck in a breath and sigh. He speaks so quietly, I barely hear him over the wind.

"AFDF. Before Fidel, I didn't feel so helpless. Now . . ."

"I know."

CHAPTER 32

After our disastrous outing three weeks ago, Serapio and I decided to take a break from fishing. We weren't very good anyway. All we ever caught was seaweed, garbage, and men running guns to Cuba. Serapio doesn't talk about going to see the men anymore, but I still feel like I have to keep him busy after school. That way he won't have time to do something stupid.

"Oye, Cumbito, this isn't right. This is cruelty to children," Serapio huffs. He grips his rake and stretches his back. "This is going to kill me."

I shake my head. "Raking shells is not going to kill you. Que dramático."

The grass in the backyard of the Reynoldses' house is littered with seashells. A year and a half ago, Hurricane Donna picked up millions of seashells out of the ocean and dumped them all over the lawns of houses in the Keys, making it impossible to mow the grass. We made a deal with Mr. Reynolds to rake the stubborn shells out of his yard and collect them in burlap sacks. He's going to pay us twenty-five cents per sack. We've collected eight so far.

Serapio tries to tie off his latest sack before it's full. I raise my eyebrow at him. "That's not going to work. Mr. Reynolds is fair."

My muscles ache as I drag the rake across the grass. The salty sea air sticks to my skin and fills my lungs with heat. The rake's metal tines clank against the hard shells. I bend down and scoop up a handful of shells into the burlap sack lying at my feet.

"Bueno, I bet I can fill a sack faster than you can," Serapio announces.

"Fine, but you have to fill it all the way. No cheating."

Serapio slaps his hands together and then winces as the blisters on his palm sting. "Contrato. Winner gets the loser's twenty-five cents."

"En sus marcas. Listos. ¡Fuera!" I shout.

Serapio and I begin raking with renewed energy. An extra twenty-five cents will feel nice in my pocket next to the caja de muertos. Trying to ignore the bullet spray of marks in the domino has been harder lately.

I haven't heard from Pepito in three weeks.

I shake my dark thoughts from my head and concentrate on collecting as many shells as I can into a pile, scooping them up with my forearms and dumping them into the burlap sack.

Mr. Reynolds told us he'd load the sacks into his truck and drive them to the Shell Factory in Key West. There the shells would be sorted, and the intact, valuable ones would be sold to tourists in the shops. The rest would be crushed and used as fill for construction projects.

Mr. Reynolds looked at us funny when he told us that tourists buy seashells to decorate their homes. I guess our eyebrows must've raised halfway up our foreheads. In Cuba, bringing seashells into your house is bad luck. That's reserved for Santero priestesses who tell your fortune. They shake the shells in a cup, toss them onto a table, and tell you, based on how they land, when you'll get married, when you'll die, and when your lost pig will finally come home.

I've got enough bad luck in my pocket right now. I don't need a conch shell in the living room adding to it.

The Reynoldses don't give me an allowance like Prima Benita did, but then again, they're providing me everything I need. But it will be nice to have money of my own. In my wildest dreams, I picture myself pulling up to Miami International Airport in a bright blue Ford Fairlane that I bought myself to pick up Pepito, Mami, Papi, and my abuelos.

I'm going to need to rake a lot of shells.

"Prepare to lose, Cumbito," Serapio taunts.

"Stop talking and rake," I shoot back.

I glance at his bag and see that it doesn't look as full as mine. For all his big talk, Serapio is too easily distracted. A seagull flying overhead, a dolphin jumping in the water, a crab crawling up the beach. His rake slows down each time he spots something more interesting than shells.

This twenty-five cents is mine. Easy.

"Que Dios me salve, mira," I hear Serapio mutter next to me.

Ay Dios mío, what does he see now?

I stand up, my back aching from being bent over. Serapio's hand rests on the top of his rake, his chin resting on his hand.

"What are you looking at?" I ask.

"Esa pelirroja," Serapio says, indicating the rocks down the shore with his chin.

I look at the pile of dark rocks, waves crashing against them, and spot a girl scrambling across the shoreline. Her hair is the brightest red I've ever seen. Like a fire in the forest.

We stand and watch her as she scampers over the rocks. She has a net tied to the waistband of her shorts. She stops suddenly and crouches down, reaching her arm between the rocks. She pulls something from a crevice, and it snaps its claws at her. I jump as she takes the crab and smashes it against the rock. Depositing it into the net hanging from her shorts, she continues climbing across the shore.

"Ay, I think I'm in love," Serapio says, pretending to stumble to the grass.

"Ay, I think you lost," I tell him, pointing to our burlap sacks.

Serapio shakes his head. "Doesn't matter."

"I thought you were going to marry a blond American."

Serapio tosses his rake aside and lies down on the grass. "I changed my mind."

I laugh and drop his half-filled sack on his stomach. He grunts and smiles.

Later that night, I lie in bed, exhausted. My muscles feel like they are pulling away from my bones, my tendons dripping off my body.

I'm tired.

My eyelids droop, and my chest falls in rhythm with the waves outside.

I dream of Mami, dancing in the kitchen to Papi's clarinet. Of Abuela twirling a soup spoon over a pot of ajiaco. Of Prima Benita racing through the streets of Miami, her white knuckles gripping the steering wheel of her car. Of Valeria standing on a chair in the middle of Royal Castle, singing at the top of her lungs.

It's only when I wake up in the morning I realize that in my dream they all had red hair.

CHAPTER 33

I can't get the song Serapio was singing all day out of my head, no matter how loud the waves are. I stand on the beach, throwing seashells into each breaking wave. Serapio's silly verse still plays in my ears.

> *Ay, pelirroja,*
> *Que venga mi pelirroja.*
> *Pelirroja, pelirroja,*
> *¿Dónde está, mi vida?*

It didn't matter that he sang his song up and down the school hallways between each class. We didn't spot the red-haired girl from the beach yesterday.

And even though I made fun of Serapio for his little song, I have to admit I was hoping to see her just as much as he was.

A large wave washes on shore, and my bare feet sink deeper into the sand as it rolls back out to the sea. I wiggle my toes, and the wet sand swirls around my legs.

"There he is," I hear a voice behind me exclaim.

I turn and see Mr. and Mrs. Reynolds walking down the beach toward me. They're gripping each other's hands tightly. I look closely at Mrs. Reynolds and notice her eyes are rimmed with red.

She's been crying.

Mr. Reynolds's lips form a tight line, and he avoids looking me in the eye.

I grip the caja de muertos in my pocket, its corners digging into my palm.

Something's wrong. I know it.

I think of Pepito and the letters I haven't gotten. Of Mami and Papi and how, no matter how hard I squint and concentrate, I can't see them across the sea.

"Please don't tell me, please don't tell me," I beg them, willing my knees not to give out and drop me onto the wet sand.

Mrs. Reynolds rushes over to me and grabs my arm to hold me up. "Oh no, dear. Nothing's wrong. Nothing's wrong at all!"

Mr. Reynolds puts his hand on my back. "Your family's coming, son. They're coming to the United States."

This time no amount of willpower keeps me from

collapsing. I dig my hands into the sand and let the sobs flow out of my throat.

Tears start to fall from Mrs. Reynolds's eyes, and she wraps her arms around me. "They're going to be safe, Cumba. You're going to see them again."

I try to say something, something even as simple as thank you. But all I see are the faces of Mami, Papi, Pepito, Abuelo, Abuela, everyone who filled my house seven months ago, before I left.

Mr. Reynolds helps me up and pats me on the back. "We knew they'd come. We knew it."

A feeling of guilt washes over me, the caja de muertos in my pocket weighing me down. I wish I could say I always had that same hope. That every single day since I set foot in the United States seven months ago, I believed for certain that my family would be with me one day.

But I didn't.

Mrs. Reynolds brushes sand off my pants. "We got word they'll be here next Wednesday. We'll drive up to Miami to meet them."

Five days. I'm going to see my family in five days. It feels unreal to even think it.

"I think this calls for a special dinner. Don't you, dear?" Mr. Reynolds says to his wife, winking.

"Oh, yes." She nods enthusiastically. "I have a huge pot of oatmeal on the stove ready to go."

I smile as Mr. Reynolds nudges my arm. I want to laugh, but the lump in my throat barely lets me breathe.

I grab Mr. Reynolds's arm before he can make his way up the beach. "My mom? My dad? Brother? Grandmother? Grandfather? Aunts? Uncles? Cousins? They are all coming?"

Mr. Reynolds sighs. "All we know for sure is that your parents and your brother are coming. That's what we were told."

I let go of Mr. Reynolds's arm. "Okay. Okay, th-thank you," I stammer.

Mr. and Mrs. Reynolds head up toward their house, their arms wrapped around each other's waists.

They're happy for me.

I turn back toward the waves and watch them advance and retreat over and over. My feet start to sink again into the sand as the water rushes against them. I close my eyes and breathe in the sea air.

I think about taking Pepito to Royal Castle for a hamburger. Fishing with Papi and Serapio. Letting Mami show Mrs. Reynolds the right way to cook Cuban food.

I shove my hands into my pockets, and my fingers wrap around the caja de muertos once again. I pull it out and hold it in my palm. The spray of dots stares up at me, taunting me.

They shout that Fidel still holds my family and won't let them go.

They scream that the sky will wrap them in darkness and that the sea will swallow them whole.

I rub my thumb over each dot.

Mami.

Papi.

Pepito.

Abuelo.

Abuela.

Manuelito.

Tía Carmen.

Tía Rosita.

Tío Enrique.

A dot for each person in my family. For each person who is my home.

"You can't have them, Fidel," I whisper to the waves. I clear my throat and lift my head. "They're not yours."

I close the caja de muertos in my fist, thrust my arm back, and launch the tile into the sea. The white rectangle bobs briefly on the surface of the water before sinking out of sight into the rolling waves.

CHAPTER 34

Querido niño,

We've been letting Pepito write to you so he would have something to do. So he wouldn't worry. But I think it's my turn now. I was the postmaster, after all. I should be in charge of the letters, no?

By now you know about what's going to happen. About who's coming to you. And you know that your abuela and I won't be there. We're too old, mi niño. Too old to start over. This has always been my country. Even with all her imperfections, she will always be my country.

I will miss you, though. Miss seeing you grow up and the man you become. I will miss teaching you how to climb a coconut tree and searching for flowers with you.

Even though we're separated by the waves, even though the sea keeps us apart, we will always be your abuelos. We will always be proud of you.

We will always love you.

Abuelo

Serapio's knee won't stop bouncing up and down in the back seat of the Reynoldses' car. He's as excited as I am, just terrible at hiding it. We're on our way to the airport, on our way to see my family. I made Serapio pinch me when we got into the car to prove to myself that it was real.

He tried to stick his finger up my nose instead.

I can barely concentrate as Mr. Reynolds winds the car through the streets of Miami. I never saw the water as we crossed the bridges in the Keys. My eyes were glued to the sky, searching for any airplane that might carry Mami, Papi, and Pepito.

I have Abuelo's letter in my pocket instead of the caja de muertos. As Mr. Reynolds drives, I run my fingers over the paper and recite Abuelo's words over and over.

"Oye, Cumbito." Serapio nudges me as we drive closer to the airport. "You think Juanita will be on the plane, too? She probably can't stand living in Cuba without me."

I shake my head. "Exactly. Your absence from Cuba is definitely her biggest problem. It's definitely not . . . anything else."

I stare at the planes flying overhead as Mr. Reynolds pulls into the airport parking lot. Serapio drones on and on about Juanita falling in love with him in Parque Vidal, and I suspect he forgot he's been obsessed with the red-haired girl since last week.

As we tumble out of the car and head into the airport, my eyes dart everywhere. What if their plane came early and they're waiting for me outside the airport? Next to that phone booth? Behind that red-and-white Chevrolet Bel Air taking up two parking spaces?

Wait.

Prima Benita? Is she here?

We enter the terminal, and a cold blast of air hits me. Every muscle in my body already twitches with excitement. The cold air just makes it worse, and I feel like I might have a seizure at any moment.

"Ay, niño, you're here!" a woman shouts to my right.

I smile and clap my hands together. Standing with her brown dress and cross necklace is Prima Benita. I look next to her and see Alejandro and his sister, as well as Valeria, still clutching the ring on her necklace.

My friends.

I run over to them and wrap Prima Benita in a hug. She buries her face in my ear, surrounding me in the scent of lavender that makes me think of Abuela and Mami.

"I prayed this day would come. Every day, I prayed," she whispers in my ear.

I think of Alejandro and me tossing the baseball methodically back and forth in her yard, and I realize I prayed for this every day, too.

Alejandro slaps me on the back, and I give him a weak punch in the arm. "Enjoying beach life?" he asks.

I nod.

Alejandro's little sister, Marisol, holds out a yellow flower to me. "I brought this for your mami," she says.

"She'll love it," I tell her.

Mr. and Mrs. Reynolds stand behind me, and I make a round of introductions. I watch them all shake hands. My best friend in Cuba, my baseball teammate and his sister, my Miami big sister, my oatmeal-making Miami mom, and the nicest people I've ever met in the Keys.

"You know, you all didn't have to come here with me," I tell them.

Valeria walks up to me and grabs my hand. "Of course we did," she says. "We're family."

I scuff my feet on the tile floor and avoid looking Valeria in the eyes, willing the knot in my throat to loosen.

We sit in the airport, and the minutes tick by. Then an hour. Mrs. Reynolds checks with an airline official, who tells us there must have been a delay.

I wring my hands so hard I almost break my fingers. What's keeping them? Why aren't they here yet?

"Oye, Cumbito," Serapio says, holding out some chocolate candies Mr. Reynolds bought for all of us at the airport shop. "You didn't tell me you were living with a goddess in Miami."

I wave off his offering. "Prima Benita?" I smirk. I know Serapio is trying to distract me.

He slaps me on the knee. "Dios mío, no. Valeria, chico."

"She's married."

Serapio raises an eyebrow at me. "You don't have to make up stories just to get me out of the way."

"I'm not. Seriously. Besides, Valeria. Juanita. La pelirroja." I hold up a finger for each girl Serapio has professed his undying and eternal love.

Serapio raises his hands in surrender. "I'm just trying to improve my odds."

I roll my eyes and stand, stretching my arms above my head. "Sin vergüenza." I laugh, lightly smacking Serapio on the back of the head.

I walk over to a large window overlooking the runway, and Valeria stands next to me. She puts her hand on my shoulder. "Don't worry. They'll be here."

I take a deep breath. "I know. I know they will."

"What's this? Is Cumba Fernandez hopeful?" She smiles and winks at me.

I feel the void in my pocket, the caja de muertos sunk to the bottom of the sea five days ago. "Yes, I guess I am." I shrug.

I watch planes roll down the runway, speed up, and take off into the air, passengers headed to places I've never seen.

In the terminal, a couple of kids stand around, their hands clutching small suitcases. Their eyes dart to every face in the airport, searching for someone unknown. I wonder if I looked that lost when I arrived at the airport seven months ago.

A voice clears behind me. "Cumba, look," Mr. Reynolds says, pointing out the window and onto the runway. A small Pan Am plane taxis down the runway and comes to a stop. I squint and try to see inside the oval windows of the plane. Is Pepito's nose pressed to the glass?

Mr. Reynolds puts his hand on my shoulder. "We have to meet them outside of customs," he says.

I realize I forgot to tell Pepito to be ready to give his name when the customs agent mumbles her English words together, *whatsyourname?*

Valeria grabs my hand and squeezes it again. I don't let go. I'm afraid if I do, I'll float up, smash into the ceiling, and break into a thousand pieces. Without the caja de muertos in my pocket, nothing weighs me down.

We walk to the waiting area outside of customs where I met Prima Benita so many months ago. Serapio bounces on his heels next to me. I wonder if he'll ever be here to see his abuela. Will Valeria get to run into Fernando's arms? I watch Alejandro wipe a tear from Marisol's face and realize they won't ever get to experience what I'm about to.

The doors to the customs area swing open, and passengers begin to file through. I scan each face, looking for Papi, Mami, and Pepito.

Finally, I see them.

Mami lets out a gasp and runs toward me, dropping her suitcase. "¡Ay, mi Cumba!"

I slam into her and wrap my arms around her waist. She kisses my head, my cheeks. She grabs my arms and pulls me away from her, examining my face. Her eyes look tired, the wrinkles at the corners a little deeper than the last time I saw her.

"Hola, Papi," I say, holding my hand out to my dad. He has a small scar under his left eye that wasn't there before. I shake my head, not wanting to think of where it came from.

"Mi niño," Papi says. "Good to see you looking so well." His voice, always so steady and calm, breaks at the end. He takes my hand and pulls me toward him, wrapping me in a hug.

I feel two small arms snake around my waist and squeeze so hard I lose my breath.

"Pepito!" I say, messing his hair and hugging him back.

"Cumba, they gave us soda on the plane! Can you believe it? And when I looked out the window, I could see so far. And I got to see where the pilot flies the plane. So many buttons and switches."

Pepito speaks so quickly he runs out of breath.

"You have plenty of time to tell me all about it."

Prima Benita steps forward and kisses Mami, Papi, and Pepito on the cheek. I introduce Valeria, Alejandro, and Marisol. Alejandro's little sister gives Mami her wilted yellow flower, and Mami thanks her with a hug.

Serapio shakes Papi's hand, and Mami gives him

a hug. "Your abuela said to take good care of you, mi niño," Mami tells him, rubbing her thumb on his cheek. Serapio smiles and looks away. I pretend not to see the tears welling up in his eyes.

Mr. Reynolds steps forward and extends his hand to Papi. "Welcome to the United States, Mr. and Mrs. Fernandez."

Papi shakes Mr. Reynolds's hand and clears his throat. "Thank you. We are happy to be here." He pauses on each word, and I can tell he's concentrating on his pronunciation.

Mrs. Reynolds introduces herself, and then she and Mami hug.

Prima Benita announces she has a special lunch prepared at her house, and we gather up suitcases and begin to head out of the airport.

I hold on to Mami. I hold on to Papi. I don't let go of Pepito. Now that they're here, I wonder if the United States will start to feel like home or if Cuba will keep tugging at my heart. Will we be able to go back? Will we ever see Abuelo and Abuela again?

I don't know.

Maybe Fidel will decide he should've been a baseball player all along and leave Cuba alone. Maybe Serapio will marry Juanita and become a decent fisherman. Maybe Pepito will achieve his dream of being an American cowboy.

Who knows? All I know is that my pockets aren't empty, even though the caja de muertos isn't there anymore. If I reach my hand in, I'll find Mami's laughter, Papi's music, Pepito's imagination, Serapio's humor. I'll wrap my hands around Mrs. Reynolds's kindness, Mr. Reynolds's intelligence, Prima Benita's faith, Alejandro's acceptance, and Valeria's friendship.

Mami, Papi, Pepito, and I walk out of the airport together with the rest of my family, the hot Miami sun filling me with hope.

AUTHOR'S NOTE

My father's passport photo

My dad, Gilberto José Cuevas, left Cuba on June 7, 1961, at the age of fifteen. Many of the events in *Cuba in My Pocket* are taken directly from stories he's told me over the years. He remembers his friends pranking their teacher, going to a German tailor for a fake passport, and soldiers shooting at American airplanes in Parque Vidal.

My abuelo and tío were able to join my dad in Miami a year after he arrived. My abuela then joined them a year later. Despite being a lawyer and a dentist in Cuba, my abuelos were not able to practice their original professions in the United States. My abuelo became a teacher and focused on working with migrant children in South Florida. My dad worked hard and gained several postgraduate degrees, teaching until retirement in the mathematics education departments of the University of Miami and Texas State University. And he ended up marrying la pelirroja, too.

Creating a fictionalized account of someone's life presents a unique set of challenges for an author, especially when that person is related to you. I hope I have done my father's story justice and captured the brave spirit of thousands of Cuban children who had the courage to flee oppression and forge lives in a new country all on their own. My prayer is that the United States will always be a welcoming refuge for those in search of freedom.

My abuelo, abuela, Tío Armando, and my dad in Miami, Florida.

PASAPORTE
PASSPORT

GLOSSARY

ajiaco—A Cuban stew with corn, potatoes, and ham. There are many varieties, and ajiaco is often a way to use up leftovers.

ajonjoli—A sesame seed candy. Sesame seeds are mixed with a sugary, simple syrup and then pressed into bars.

azabache—A gemstone worn on a bracelet or necklace. It is typical for Cuban babies to wear an azabache to keep away bad luck.

batido—A milkshake. The most common batidos are guava or mamey, both types of fruit.

Bay of Pigs invasion—Occurred April 17–19, 1961. It was an attempt by the United States and Cuban exiles to remove Fidel Castro from power. Due to lack of proper support from the US, the exiles were defeated.

bocadito—A sandwich. The most common type would be made with baguette-style bread, ham, and cheese.

cocotazo—A smack on the back of the head.

crema de leche—Milk cream. A type of caramel candy.

croquetas—Minced ham, breaded and fried.

el cucuy—An urban legend common in many latin countries, similar to the boogeyman.

encantado—Pleasure to meet you.

galletas—Cookies.

garrison—A collective term for any body of troops stationed at a particular location.

"Guantanamera"—A popular song in Cuba based on a poem by José Martí, a Cuban national hero.

hasta la victoria, siempre—"Until Victory, always." A well-known saying by Che Guevara, an Argentine revolutionary who fought with Fidel Castro to oust President Batista.

Judge Advocate General—The unit to which a military lawyer is assigned.

mal de ojo—The evil eye. Many Cuban superstitions are meant to keep away the evil eye.

mal rayo me parta—Literally, "May bad lightning strike me." A way of swearing the truth.

me resbala—Literally, "It slips me." This is a way of saying that something doesn't matter to you, as if it just slips off your skin.

patria o muerte—Literally, "Fatherland or death." One of the many slogans of Castro's regime.

picadillo—A mixture of ground beef and spices. Depending on the region and family, it may include potatoes, raisins, and/or olives. Typically served over white rice.

President Batista—A Cuban military officer who served as Cuba's president from 1940 to 1944 and as its US-supported dictator from 1952 to 1959 before being overthrown by Fidel Castro's forces.

Radio Rebelde—A Cuban radio station controlled by the government.

sana sana, colita de rana—A rhyme many Spanish-speakers learn when they are little. It means "Heal, heal, little frog tail."

te lo juro—Literally, "I promise you."

tocororo—The national bird of Cuba, its red, white, and blue coloring matching the Cuban flag.

venceremos—Literally, "We will overcome." Another slogan of Castro's regime.

Yanqui—Yankee. A way to refer to someone from the United States.

yuca—A starchy vegetable similar to a potato. Often boiled and served with garlic sauce.

yuma—Refers to someone who is foreign-born. Catholic priests born outside Cuba were referred to as "yuma priests."

ACKNOWLEDGMENTS

Every book an author writes is a labor of love, but *Cuba in My Pocket* is a piece of my heart. This story took on even greater meaning for me when my father passed nine months before its publication. So many people came alongside me in support and love. I am forever grateful for them.

My agent, Stefanie Sanchez Von Borstel of Full Circle Literary, who not only expertly champions my stories and my career, but supports me as a friend. You are the only person I will willingly talk on the phone with.

My editor, Trisha de Guzman at FSG/Macmillan, who cried with me each time we read over this book, who cheered with me as I accomplished new things, who enthusiastically boosts and supports my stories. You are an author's dream come true.

Cynthia Lliguichuzhca, who works tirelessly on my behalf. Trisha Previte, whose gorgeous design brought this book to life. Kristen Luby, Mary Van Akin, and the rest of the amazing Macmillan team, who cheer me on.

I am indebted to fellow Cuban American authors whose books chronicling our culture inspired me: Alma

Flor Ada, Ruth Behar, Carlos Eire, Margarita Engle, Enrique Flores-Galbis, and Cristina D. Gonzalez.

My Las Musas hermanas, Austin author community, Pitch Wars friends, and Spooky Middle Grade ghouls who showed me how incredible the writing world is. You've made this introvert feel welcomed.

Sarah Kapit, who was the first to read this story and gave me the bravery to tell it. Thank you for your continued support and for always making me feel like I'm on the right track. I love working with you.

Natalia Goldberg and Lori Keckler, whose friendship during one of the most difficult years of my life grounded me. Our never-ending text threads about everything and nothing sustain me. Abrazos, amigas!

Amparo Ortiz, whose all-caps texts about K-pop I will forever cherish. Thank you for giving me joy when I was at my lowest and for being mi hermana en corazón.

My cousins Manolo and Nora Delosantos, who entrusted me with their stories.

Mom, Heather, and Rob, who cheer me on and support me no matter what.

Joe and Soren, who fill my heart with joy. I wouldn't have any books to write if it weren't for the two of you. Thank you for always loving me.

And finally, to Dad, who was my best friend. I'll always strive to make you proud as I honor your legacy with my stories.